The Long Way Around

By Shelley Banks

Chapter One

Andie looked at the clothes on the bed and groaned. She'd have to sort through them for the third time. There were still too many to fit into the wardrobe in the caravan. How was she supposed to pick such a limited amount of clothes to last a year? Whatever she chose, she'd probably be sick of in six months. But buying new clothes while travelling around Australia was not within the budget. There were a lot of things that weren't in the budget, but Andie pushed those thoughts aside. They weren't going to back out now, not with the caravan on the driveway and the route mapped out.

As she stared at her clothes, she wondered if Jennifer was having the same problem. Although, given the size of Jennifer's walk-in wardrobe, she suspected it would be more challenging for her. Andie's two-door closet could fit into the corner of Jennifer's wardrobe.

It took her another hour to sort her clothes, but finally, it was done. Then it was on to the next thing to pack. It would have been easier if Craig had been helping, but he hadn't shown much interest in packing. All he was interested in was checking the car and the caravan. Again. For the sixth time. Rob would be doing the same. Robert, she corrected herself. He didn't like being called Rob anymore. Not for a few years now. Checking everything repeatedly to make sure it was perfect was more Robert's personality than Craig's. But if the subject came up,

Craig wouldn't want there to be any suggestion that he hadn't put in as much effort in preparing for the trip as Robert had. Andie watched through the window as Craig tested the indicators and the brake lights, checked the tow bar, and made sure all the hatches were closed. She thought about going outside and asking again for his help packing but decided to let it go. It would be easier to do it herself.

As she went from room to room, checking the contents of cupboards and drawers, making sure there was nothing she hadn't already pulled out to pack, she took notice of all the details of the house that had been theirs for the past seventeen years. It wasn't as big as Jennifer and Robert's, but it was big enough for what they needed. Andie would have liked a few things fixed, though, things that she'd been asking about for years, things that Craig never found the time to do. Whenever she looked at the window that wouldn't shut properly, the missing shelf in the hall cupboard, and the broken door on the oven, she thought she might try to fix them herself. But she already did more than her fair share of the chores. If she took those on, it would give Craig an excuse to do less than he did now. And besides, he was a builder. He could fix those things in a tenth of the time it would take her.

Andie remembered when they built the house. Their budget didn't extend to more than a single-storey, three-bedroom home. However, the other bedrooms were never used for their intended purpose.

Back then, the walls were freshly painted, and the carpets were new, as was the furniture. Now, as she stood in the lounge room, the couch she was looking at should have been replaced by now, along with the TV cabinet they'd bought all those years ago. The curtains in the bedrooms were the same. Over the years, they'd updated the kitchen and bought a new dining room table. But even though they'd talked about renovating the rest of the house, something always came up, and the money they'd saved was spent elsewhere. Like the trip they were about to embark on. Heading into the bathroom, she sighed at the dated colour scheme and the splintered crack that adorned one of the mirror's corners. She gazed at her reflection. She'd had her light brown hair cut in preparation for the trip, and now it fell to the top of her shoulders rather than further down her back as it had for years. She tucked her hair behind her ears and looked at the details on her face—hazel eyes with only a couple of fine lines at the crease and high cheekbones that had always added a definition to her face that she liked. She continued to look, moving down, and was pleased that she still had the same slim figure she'd always had. So far, the middle-aged spread had left her alone. Andie took one last look in the mirror and went back to packing.

'The caravan is right to go,' Craig said as he came back inside, interrupting her thoughts.

Of course it is, Andie said to herself. She wasn't in the mood to have the same conversation for the fourth day in a row.

She also didn't think Craig would take too kindly to her thoughts about why he kept checking the caravan.

'You're not taking all those clothes, are you?' Craig said, looking down at the bed.

'Yes, I am. And that's not a lot of outfits.'

'Looks like a lot to me, although Jennifer's probably taking more.'

Andie glared at him but didn't say a word. Instead, she walked to the spare room and continued sorting through what was there. But Craig followed.

'We don't need to pack another blanket,' he said as Andie started folding. 'We're not going to Antarctica.'

'But we are going to the desert, and it gets cold at night.'

'We won't get there for two and a half months. It's only the beginning of April. If we need another blanket, we can buy one.'

Andie sighed. Is that with our unlimited funds, she thought to herself. She knew how touchy Craig was about the subject of money. And especially the difference between their finances and those of their travelling companions.

'Have you decided what clothes you're taking?'

Craig shook his head.

'We're leaving tomorrow. Why don't you do that now.'

And leave me in peace for a while, Andie thought as she watched him walk out of the room. The trip had been his idea, yet she'd done most of the work getting ready for it. He seemed to have no concept of everything they'd need to get them through the next twelve months, except for the BBQ. That was one of the first things to go into the storage area of the caravan. That and the fishing rods.

'Did you get the mail redirected?' Craig called out.

'Yes.'

'What about cancelling the paper?'

'Did that too.'

'And you've organised someone to look after the garden?'

'Yes, of course. What about your to-do list?'

'Everything's done.'

Andie very much doubted that. 'Just pack your clothes.'

'What about food? How much are we taking?'

'Everything that's left in the fridge.'

Andie heard him leave their bedroom and go into the kitchen.

'We don't need all this.'

'We can't leave it here,' Andie said as she walked into the kitchen and saw him staring at the fridge contents.

'Can't we just get rid of it?'

'There's nothing wrong with it. We're not throwing out perfectly good food.'

'It can't be worth that much.'

'That's not the point. It's a waste. And how would you know how much those things cost? I can't remember the last time you did the grocery shopping.'

'I do plenty of other things,' Craig said as he shut the fridge door. 'I'll let you sort all that out.'

'Not going to help?'

'I've already given you my suggestion, and you didn't like it.'

I'll add that to my list of things to do, Andie muttered under her breath as Craig walked out of the kitchen. Long after he'd gone, she was still thinking about his lack of help in getting ready for the trip, only focusing on what was important to him. But it wasn't just getting ready to go. Andie couldn't remember the last time Craig focused on something important to her, either as an individual or a couple.

That night, Andie lay awake, staring at the ceiling. This would be the last night she would sleep in her bed for three hundred and sixty-five days. Beside her, Craig was snoring. Usually, when he snored, she went to another room to sleep, but because this was the last night, she wanted to spend it in her own bed. She wasn't sure what she'd do in the caravan—there was nowhere to go if Craig snored. And the bed in the van is only a double. They'd had a king bed all their married life, and she liked the space between them. She found it hard to sleep if someone was touching her. It was one of the many questions her sister had asked when they'd been talking about the trip.

'Twelve months...really, Andrea?' Camila had said. 'You're going to leave your life behind for twelve months?'

Andie had never liked the name Andrea and had been shortening it since she was a teenager. Camila was the only one who still called her by her proper name.

'I'm not leaving my life behind. I'm living it. Haven't you ever wanted to go on an adventure?'

'I go on adventures all the time. We go overseas every year.'

'Staying at a 5-star resort and spending your time at the day spa is not what I meant by adventure.'

'I'd rather stay in a 5-star resort than a caravan. How much room are you going to have? I imagine the bed is small. How are you going to sleep in something smaller than what you're used to?'

Andie had assured Camila that there would be plenty of room and that she'd be fine with the sleeping arrangements. But even as she'd said it, she hadn't been so sure. And it wasn't just the sleeping arrangements. Everything would be different. Was she as ready for this adventure as she initially thought?

Like Andie, Jennifer was also staring at her clothes. She'd never really taken much notice of the size of her walk-in wardrobe before. But now that she was trying to sort out what to bring, she realised how many clothes she had. And wondered why she'd bought so many. Like all the expensive dresses she'd worn once. Her work suits were the only items that got worn regularly. And none of those would be coming with her. As she looked at them, she wondered what it was going to be like not going into the office for the next twelve months. Jennifer had been working since she graduated from university the first time around, so this was a big change. But it was one she was looking forward to. It would be an adventure, something she hadn't had in a long time. And it would be a good chance to spend more time with Robert. Their careers had been taking precedence over their relationship in the past few years, and it was time to change that.

Clothes weren't the only thing occupying Jennifer's mind as she packed. The more she looked at the caravan and then looked back at the house, she couldn't ignore the vast size difference between them. At first, when the trip had been suggested, she'd liked the idea of downsizing for a year and only taking the essentials. But it turned out there were many essentials in their double-storey, four-bedroom, four-car garage, two entertaining areas and three-bathroom house. The more she looked, the more confused she got about what to take and what to leave behind. They were going the next morning, and she still had to ring the pool company to check if someone would be coming out regularly to maintain the pool. At least she'd organised for her sister to come around occasionally and start her car while they were gone. She'd bought her brand-new BMW the day she'd received her last promotion, and every time she drove it, she felt proud of everything she'd achieved in her career. The brand new Landcruiser they'd bought for the trip was nice to drive and had all the bells and whistles a 4WD could possibly have, but she would miss driving her car. She was still thinking about her BMW when she realised Robert was standing behind her.

'How's your packing going?'

Jennifer turned to look at him. 'Almost done. What about you?'

'Finished, and everything is in the caravan.'

Jennifer smiled to herself. She wasn't surprised. He'd probably finished putting everything in its place days ago.

'Would you like me to help with your packing?'

Jennifer shook her head. He'd already made several suggestions about what she should pack, suggestions she'd tactfully ignored. She'd become good at ignoring his suggestions over the years. In the background, she could hear his phone ring. She left him to answer it, and as he began talking, she started wandering through the house. As much as she loved what they had, a part of her was looking forward to getting back to basics. Once she'd sorted out the packing, that is. It would be just like when she and Robert got together. Before the trappings that came with their money, when it was just the two of them in their first small house together. Before either of them went back to university and changed careers. She'd been thinking about that time a lot lately and was surprised at how much she missed it. And how much the state of her relationship with Robert left niggling doubts in her mind.

The next morning, after they'd eaten breakfast and done the dishes, Andie and Craig did one last check of each room, making sure the windows were shut and the lights were turned off. Then they closed and locked the front door.

'Let's go,' Craig said. 'I can't wait to get on the road.'

Before closing the front door, Andie picked up her laptop. She'd left it on the hall table near the door, so she didn't forget it. Although she wanted to limit her screen time while they were away, she'd somehow been talked into doing a travel blog. Jennifer thought it would be an excellent way to document the trip and let their friends and family know what they were up to and where they'd gone. And it would be, but Andie knew that once they were on the road, she would be responsible for writing most of the posts while Jennifer would take the accompanying photos. In Jennifer's words, it made sense that Andie, as the English teacher, did most of the writing.

Andie took one last look at the house as Craig backed out of the driveway. Too late now, she thought to herself. She didn't know what the next twelve months would bring, and she felt a slight sense of unease, one she couldn't pinpoint the cause of.

'Are you ready, Jennifer,' Robert called out.

It was at that moment she decided. She'd gone by Jennifer since she was promoted from HR Director to Executive Director of People and Culture at the firm she worked for. But with twelve months of holidays in front of them, she wanted to go by the more casual Jen. Like she used to. Robert would still call her Jennifer, but that was just his way. He didn't like his name being shortened anymore, so she doubted he'd shorten hers.

'Almost. Just give me five minutes.'

As she brushed her teeth, she looked at herself in the mirror. She loved the new shade of chestnut her hairdresser had used. It brought out the green in her eyes. And like Andie, she too had escaped the middle-aged spread, retaining the slim figure she'd always had. They were similar in shape, the only difference being that Jen was a couple of centimetres taller. Not that Andie was short. They were both in the average height range.

Finishing with her teeth, she put her toothbrush in her toiletries bag and walked out to the caravan, ready to tackle the dilemma she'd been avoiding. Trying to get all the food into the caravan fridge and freezer. There was no way it was going to fit. She sighed, then picked up the phone and called Andie.

'Do you have any room in your freezer?'

'No, and we've just left. Why?'

'I've bought too much meat.'

'Of course you did.'

'I was just being prepared. I'll have to give what won't fit to the neighbours. I can't leave meat in the freezer at home for a year. I'll see you soon.'

After delivering the excess meat to their neighbours and saying goodbye, Jen headed back to the caravan just in time to see Robert checking that everything was ready for the trip one more time before they headed off. As well as having a mechanic go over their car with a fine-tooth comb, he'd also taken the caravan back to the dealership to make sure everything was in working order. Jen couldn't see the need as they'd only had the van for three months. But Robert insisted. Just as he'd insisted on checking everything himself, over and over since they'd brought it home, even though he wasn't the slightest bit mechanically minded. Inside the caravan, Jen added one more jacket to the clothes already there. Robert's clothes had either been hung up in order of length or folded neatly in piles by clothing type. Jen's things weren't quite as neat, but somewhere along the way, Robert would rearrange them. He'd start being subtle about it—moving one or two things—then give up and do it all at once. Jen had learned long ago just to let him do it. It wasn't worth the fight that would ensue. But lately, she hadn't wanted to let it go as she had for so long.

When Craig first mentioned the trip idea all those months ago, Robert had said he'd be happy to leave something like that to Craig and Andie. But Jen liked the idea and began bringing it up in conversation, saying how much fun they would have and what a great experience it would be. And how it would be a fantastic opportunity to spend time together and reconnect.

Robert eventually came around to her way of thinking, and before they knew it, plans were made, and they had a start date.

'We should be right on time to meet Craig and Andie,' Robert said from the driver's seat.

Robert had suggested they meet at a rest stop just north of the city and then head off on their journey together.

'Everything is secure in the caravan,' Robert said. 'And I've double-checked to make sure we haven't left anything behind. We shouldn't need further supplies during the trip other than food.'

'That's good,' Jen said.

Robert nodded. 'A little bit of preparation goes a long way.'

'I'm glad we're finally leaving,' Jen said, trying not to smile at Robert's words.

Robert nodded. 'Me too. I know I wasn't on board at the beginning, but I'm glad I gave it some thought and changed my mind.'

After a lot of prompting, Jen thought to herself as she crossed her fingers down by her side, where Robert couldn't see. Crossing them, hoping they would reconnect and get back to where Jen wanted them to be. She wasn't sure where it would leave her if they didn't. Or them.

As they got to the city outskirts, Jen wound down the window to feel the autumn air. All the stress she'd felt from her job these past few years began to fade away.

'There's Craig and Andie,' Robert said, looking straight ahead.

Jen picked up her phone and texted Andie.

I can't believe we're on our way.

I know!

See you soon at the rest stop.

Chapter Two

Andie and Jen jumped out of their cars at the same time and hugged each other, their excited words spilling out before they untangled themselves. Craig and Robert shook hands. As Andie watched them, she was struck by how different they looked. Craig was tall and fit with broad shoulders from all the years of doing a physical job. And the sun continued to bleach his sandy-coloured hair. Although now, it had flecks of grey. Robert was shorter and slightly overweight, thanks to the corporate lunches he went to as a project manager. His reddish-brown hair didn't show any grey, but maybe that was hidden underneath. Or maybe he had some help in covering it.

'That was good timing,' Robert said. 'You coming right behind us on the highway.'

'Yes, I guess it is,' Craig replied.

'Are you still happy to drive to Hervey Bay today?' Robert asked.

Craig nodded. 'I'm looking forward to going to Fraser Island tomorrow. I haven't been.'

'You'll like it,' Robert said. 'It's a great spot. I've got us tickets for the boat and the full-day tour.'

Craig turned to look at him. 'I thought we were getting them in Hervey Bay.'

'Didn't want to miss out. Just in case the boat or the tour was full.'

'I can't imagine either being full on a Tuesday.'

'You never know.'

'How much do we owe you?'

'Tickets for the boat were $35 each. The full-day tour was $239 each. Very reasonable, I thought.'

Andie watched them as they talked. Over five hundred dollars on the second day of the trip. She mentally went through the weekly budget she'd set. They'd be fine as long as there were no more expensive tickets that week. And besides, she was looking forward to going to Fraser Island too. She'd last visited over twenty years ago during the brief time she and Craig were apart. She remembered that time vividly. Remembered how she thought she was too young to be in a serious relationship, even though she and Craig had been together since high school. But high school was different to being an adult, to living with someone. So, she'd ended things with Craig, thinking she should see other guys before settling down. Guys like those she'd met at university who had other interests apart from football and beer. One of those guys was Toby. A nice guy she always had fun with. But it soon turned out that was all he wanted to do. Have fun. All the time. Eventually, Andie decided she couldn't keep up with the constant partying, so she ended it. But not before the trip to Fraser Island. With Toby, everything had to be the best.

So he'd organised one of the finest rooms available, booked them on a private tour of the island and made reservations at the restaurant every night. It was a great trip, but by the end, the constant movement and the need to be doing something left her feeling tired.

Not long after she broke up with him, she saw Craig one day, and soon they were back together. Something about him was familiar, and how they were together felt comfortable. But were familiar and comfortable things to build a life on?

'Shall we head off?' Craig asked.

Jen nodded. 'Absolutely. Let's go.'

Andie smiled as she looked at Jen. It was nice to see her so happy. It had been a while since Andie had last seen her like that. Although there was something underneath her smile that Andie couldn't put her finger on. She'd known Jen since primary school, and she'd always been joyful and carefree. But she'd been different in the past few years since the new job. Andie still wasn't sure whether Jen had chosen to change careers because she wanted to or because she thought she should. Or because Robert thought they should have more than they did.

'Why did he buy those tickets?' Craig asked as soon as they got in the car. 'It's not what we talked about.'

'Yes, but you know what he's like. I'm sure he meant well.'

'I don't know about that. Rob's always trying to take over everything.'

Andie sighed. 'Let it go. And don't call him Rob. You know he hates that.'

'I'll call him whatever I like when he can't hear me.'

As they started to pull out, Robert managed to get in front.

'See, I told you,' Craig said. 'He had to go first.'

'Or maybe he was ready before you.'

Craig didn't reply.

The highway wasn't busy heading north. But heading south, the cars were moving at a snail's pace towards the city, and Andie was glad she wasn't going that way. For the next twelve months, there would be no 5.30 am alarms, no daily commute in peak hour traffic, and no trying to fit all the things she enjoyed into the few hours she had left between work and household chores. The more she thought about it, the more her misgivings about the trip began to fade.

They didn't need to stop for anything, and four hours later, both cars pulled into Hervey Bay. The caravan park had plenty of spots available, so they had their pick.

Robert wound down the driver's side window. 'I think we should set up a couple of rows back to protect our cars and caravans from the salt air.'

Craig did the same, then shook his head through the open window. 'There aren't many trees between the caravan park and the beach, so we won't get any protection.'

'But what about the wind?' Robert said. 'I don't want to feel the caravan rocking while I'm trying to sleep.'

Craig smirked. 'The caravan should be rocking before you go to sleep.'

Andie could tell by the look on Robert's face that he wasn't pleased by Craig's comment.

'I meant by the wind.' Robert said.

'Don't think it will matter. As I said, there's no protection. So we may as well set up in the spots with the best view of the ocean.'

As Craig said it, he started backing the caravan into the spot he'd chosen.

'We won't be here long enough to set up the annex,' he said once the caravan was in place.

'No, but it would be nice to have some shade,' Andie said. 'The view is lovely, and it would be nice to sit and look at it later today when the sun is going down.'

While Craig was rolling out the blind from the side of the caravan, Andie stared out at the water. She'd always been soothed by the sight of the ocean. Beside them, Robert had reversed their van into the spot next to Andie and Craig. Unfortunately, it didn't have the same view.

'Looks like we'll be having drinks outside your van,' Jen called out.

'Happy to be the hosts,' Craig called back.

Robert looked around. 'Great place to stop for our first night. Shame the shower block is between us and the beach.'

'We can see around it,' Jen said. 'And besides, we're only here for two nights. Today's almost over, and tomorrow we'll be on Fraser Island all day.'

'I'll pull our blind out anyway. We can have breakfast under it tomorrow.'

When both couples had set up, Robert pulled out a bottle of French champagne.

'It's our first day. We must celebrate.'

'I'll stick with beer,' Craig said.

'You can't toast with beer,' Robert said. 'I'm sure you can manage one. Save the beer for later.'

Andie turned back to look at the ocean. She didn't need to look in Craig's direction. She already knew what the look on his face would be. He didn't like champagne, something Robert was aware of. But on this occasion, Andie wished Craig would just go with the flow for once. Even if he had one sip and then gave the rest to her. This was the beginning of their year-long trip around Australia, and it deserved to be celebrated.

'But not too much beer later,' Jen said. 'I can't imagine being hungover on the boat would feel good. Or staying up too late and being tired.'

Craig nodded. 'I went on a deep-sea fishing trip once with some guys from work after we'd been out late the night before. There wasn't one of us who wasn't sick over the side.'

'That's a charming story,' Jen said. 'And staying up late doesn't mean we have to drink as well.'

'Of course it does,' Robert said. 'It's our first night. We've got plenty of champagne.'

Andie looked at Craig, silently telling him to behave.

'One champagne now and then beers after that,' Craig said.

'To our trip,' Robert said once everyone had a glass.

'To our trip,' the others chorused.

It didn't take long for the bottle to go and for Robert to reach for another one.

'Why don't we go for a walk,' Jen said. 'Look around a bit.'

Andie nodded. 'That would be good, especially after sitting in the car all morning.'

'Why don't you two head off, and we'll catch up,' Robert said. 'I want to check everything's set up correctly with the caravan. I'm sure Craig wants to do the same.'

Jen and Andie had only walked about thirty metres before Jen started laughing.

'Pretty sure Craig doesn't need to check the caravan again.'

Andie laughed too. 'No, he doesn't.'

'Robert means well. He just likes things to be perfect.'

'I know. And Craig will be fine,' Andie said aloud. Eventually, she added under her breath.

As they walked along the esplanade, Jen researched Hervey Bay on her phone.

'Apparently, we're 290 kilometres from home,' she said. 'It's a natural bay between the Queensland mainland and Fraser Island. Whale watching is big. Pity we're out of season for that. I've always wanted to go whale watching. What else does it say? Hervey Bay has a mild climate, averaging 30 degrees in summer and 22 degrees in winter. If we want to go shopping while we're here, we need to go to Pialba. That's where the shopping centre is. For dinner, most of the restaurants are in Scarness and Torquay as well as Shelley Beach.'

Andie laughed again. 'Very comprehensive. Thank you for that information.'

Jen smiled. 'Any time. And there's the information for our first blog post.'

Their blog, *The Long Way Around.* Andie wrote the first entry that afternoon using the information Jen had found.

After putting her phone away, Jen fell silent for a few minutes, thinking about what they were doing – the trip, not the blog. Although she should think about that too, seeing as it was her idea. They'd only just left, and Robert had started rearranging things while they were setting up. He was probably doing that again now. There was nothing wrong with how they'd packed the van, but he couldn't leave things alone. Except her. She couldn't remember the last time they'd done something together. For Robert, the only thing that mattered was his career. Which, to be fair, was how she'd felt for the past few years. But not anymore. She needed things to change. She no longer wanted her life to be so one-sided. What she wanted was a balance between her work and her relationship. She just hoped Robert would come to the same conclusion. That hope had been on her mind longer than she wanted to admit.

His words at the caravan park were on her mind as well. Even though he liked everything to be perfect, it didn't mean everyone else did. Or that his idea of perfect was the same as other people's. It was often different from her own view. He'd once listened to what she had to say and considered her opinions and feelings before making decisions. Now what she thought had slipped down the rung of things he took into consideration.

As Jen looked out at the water, she realised that if their relationship didn't change on this trip, then when it was over, there wouldn't be a relationship. Twelve months. Surely that was enough time to turn things around because that's what she wanted.

When they'd first met, his desire to better himself was something Jen admired. She remembered the night he'd told her about his family, living week to week, going without one thing to pay for another. There had never been a shortage of love, but there had been a shortage of material possessions. Which shouldn't have mattered as much as it did, but when his friends started getting the popular brand of bicycle or boardshorts, and all his parents could afford were the low-cost brands, it mattered more than Robert had wanted to acknowledge.

He'd only talked about that aspect of his childhood once. Whenever she'd asked him about it after that, he clammed up and wouldn't divulge anything more. Jen often wondered if his focus on money was because he feared finding himself, once more, having very little.

As they continued to walk, Jen told herself to put her thoughts aside and pull her attention back to what was happening around her. She may never come back here, so she should pay attention to everything she can see and hear. Although a glance at Andie made Jen think she was distracted, too.

The more they walked, first along the waterfront, then through the streets of the town, the more Andie thought about where she came from. She'd always lived in Brisbane—born there, raised there, bought a house there. But lately, she'd started to feel like it was too busy. Every time she drove somewhere, the roads were congested, and it took her longer to get where she was going. She had to wait longer at the supermarket checkout to pay for their groceries. The footpaths in the CBD had more people on them than ever, and she found she was always being swallowed up in a crowd. The pace she was walking dictated by whether the crowd was moving quickly or slowly. She tried to avoid going into the city centre, but if she needed to pick something up, it was the closest place near the school where she taught.

Here, she could walk at her own pace. She didn't feel rushed or held back. There were cars on the road, but none of them seemed in a hurry, and no one was tooting their horn. In the cafes, people talked to each other instead of staring at their phones or laptops. Even the supermarket queues were short. Although they'd only been in town for two hours, Andie felt like she was slowing down.

'You two haven't walked as far as I thought you would've by now,' Craig said as he and Robert caught up with them.

And just like that, Andie's peace started to dissipate.

'There's a lot to see,' Jen said. 'And I've been taking photos.'

'Did she tell you she's going to take photos everywhere we go?' Robert asked.

Andie nodded.

'I don't want to forget the places we visit,' Jen said. 'And besides, we need them for the blog.'

Andie smiled. 'As well as taking photos, Jen's been telling me about the town.'

Jen gave Robert and Craig a quick update on what she'd learned.

'Trust you to find out where the shopping is,' Craig said.

Andie punched him lightly in the arm. 'That was just one thing,' she said. 'Why did you have to go straight there?'

'It's all right,' Jen said. 'I'm sure he was just joking.'

I'm not sure he was, Andie muttered under her breath. Just because Jen often turned up wearing new clothes, Craig seemed to think all she did when she wasn't working was shop. Andie would have loved new clothes more often if they could afford them. Craig didn't care what he wore. As long as his clothes didn't have holes, he was happy. Although that only applied to the clothes he wore when they went out. Most of the clothes he wore around the house had holes in them. Clothes that should have been thrown away years ago, but he never wanted to.

'Let's have another toast,' Robert said a few minutes after they arrived back at their caravans just before sunset. 'The first one was too quick.'

Craig opened a beer before Robert could pour him another champagne. Then he walked over to the table where Jen had placed some nibbles and started eating.

Andie sighed. He could have waited until they all had a drink. Then Andie stopped herself. They were spending every day of the next twelve months together. She had to stop feeling annoyed by some of the things Craig did.

When he'd finished pouring, Robert handed Jen and Andie a glass.

'Here's to our trip, for the second time,' he said. 'May it be full of adventures and great memories.'

'And no accidents or dramas,' Craig added.

'Don't say that,' Jen said. 'Now I'm worried.'

'Nothing to worry about,' Robert said. 'We'll be fine.'

'I just wanted to remind us that we need to be careful,' Craig said. 'We'll be driving long distances on extended, straight stretches of road with nothing around us.'

Andie was about to glare at him when she remembered her thoughts from a moment ago. And besides, he was right. But this probably wasn't the right time to mention it. So, instead, she asked what they should do for dinner.

'I think we should go out,' Jen said. 'It's our first night. We should go somewhere nice.'

It was only the first night, and Andie was thinking about their budget for the second time in a few hours. She should have suggested they stay where they were instead of asking the question.

'We'll go to one of those restaurants we saw on our walk,' Robert said. 'But first, let's finish this champagne. I can't remember the last time I had champagne on a Monday.'

'That's because it's usually wine,' Jen said. 'And you and I don't get home from work until 7 pm. I still can't believe we're not going to be doing that for the next year.'

At 7 pm last Monday, Craig was on to his fourth beer, Andie thought, while she was in the kitchen cooking dinner, tired after a long day at work.

'I'm looking forward to not working for a while,' Andie said.

In all the years she'd worked, Andie had never taken any extended time off. As much as she loved her job, the thought that she wouldn't be standing in front of a classroom full of students for the next twelve months was nice. Most days, she loved her job, but it was hard when she was tired or wasn't feeling well. She would miss the students, though. She'd taught them through the first term and got to know them. By the time she got back, they would have moved on. Some would be in their first semester of university; others would be working. Some would still be trying to figure out what they wanted to do. But, whatever they ended up doing, she hoped they would all be ok. And that they remembered at least some of what she'd taught them and, hopefully, gained a love of reading from the books she'd set them.

As they sat in the chairs, looking at the ocean, Andie opened her laptop and began typing.

The Long Way Around

The beginning – our trip is underway! We drove from Brisbane to Hervey Bay on day 1. It was an easy drive, and we didn't encounter much traffic heading north. We can't believe we're finally on our way after months of planning.

Andie looked up to ask Jen to send her the information on Hervey Bay that she'd found. Once she had it, she copied and pasted it into the blog. She also uploaded some of Jen's photos and then clicked the save button. The first entry was done.

Jen had been watching Andie type the entry and knew she should have done more than just forward information and a few photos. Even though it had been her idea, she'd assumed that Andie would do most of the writing. She was much better at it than Jen was. Unless it was one of the many proposals, reports, presentations or emails she drafted at work. She'd become quite adept at getting her point across in a way that all other points of view seemed insignificant in comparison.

When she'd first told her colleagues about her decision to take a twelve-month leave of absence and travel the country, they thought she was joking. In an office where career was the number one focus for everyone, which until recently had included Jen, no one could understand what she was doing. Or why she'd take that much time off. Things would change while she was away. What if the person stepping into her role didn't want to give it back when the time came?

That thought had occurred to Jen too. Although, given her experience, and the things she knew about the company after working there for so long, she knew it wouldn't be hard to step back into the same role. But that was also what was bothering her—stepping back. What was the point of experiencing a whole new way of life and all that it entailed, only to go back to exactly what she had before? She didn't want that for her marriage, and she wasn't sure she wanted that for her career either. Not for the first time that day, she thought about how much she was counting on this trip to fix all the things that were wrong.

To distract herself from her thoughts, she picked up her phone and read what Andie had posted on the blog. And clicked the like button straight away. It wasn't much of a contribution, and she would tell Andie what a great job she'd done, but she would try and make more of an effort on the next entry.

Before leaving for dinner, they all headed into their caravans to get changed.

'How will I put up with him for the next twelve months?' Craig fumed.

Andie sighed. 'He's not that bad.'

'Always has to have everything his way.'

'He was just trying to have a small celebration to honour the occasion. Don't worry about it now. We have to get ready.'

And stop acting like a child, she muttered under her breath. This trip was your idea in the first place.

Twenty minutes later, they were walking along Charlton Esplanade for the second time that day.

'We're coming up to the restaurants I saw,' Robert said.

Jen took hold of his hand. 'How about Andie and Craig pick which one we go to.'

Andie smiled at her in response before jumping in and picking one. If she left it to Craig, he'd probably pick one he knew Robert wouldn't like. And if it had been up to Robert, he would have chosen the most expensive one.

The restaurant Andie chose was Italian, and the food was delicious. Even Robert couldn't fault it. The two waiters, Malcolm and John, were interested in what they were doing, so they stayed until closing to answer their questions.

'So, you're travelling all the way around the country?' Malcolm asked.

Craig nodded.

'For the next twelve months?'

Craig nodded again. 'That's the plan.'

'I've always wanted to do that,' John said.

'Why don't you?' Robert asked.

'Two school-aged children. Twelve months is too long to take them away from their classes.'

'You could teach them,' Andie said. 'I'm a teacher, and I've had students who've travelled with their parents, and I've provided them with material to use.'

John shook his head. 'You see what I do for a job. I don't think teaching is up my alley.'

'What about your wife?' Jen asked.

'She passed away.'

'I'm sorry to hear that,' Jen said, her eyes fixed on him as he spoke.

The grief was visible on his face. Jen couldn't imagine what it would be like to have your spouse pass away while you were still young. Maybe when more time had passed, John wouldn't have that sad look on his face when he spoke about his wife, but for now, it was firmly in place.

'So what route are you taking?' Malcolm asked. 'North, I assume, seeing as you're here.'

Robert nodded. 'Yes, that's right. We're heading up as far as Mackay, and then we're going inland to Longreach. Then we'll go up through Winton to Cloncurry before heading east through Hughenden and Charters Towers and then back to the coast at Townsville.'

'You've put a lot of thought into that,' Malcolm said. 'There's a lot to see in the north and west of Queensland.'

Andie nodded. 'And we're looking forward to seeing as much as we can.'

'Sounds like a good plan,' John said. 'But you'll miss going through Bowen. That's where I'm from. It's a nice town.'

'You're right,' Craig said. 'Maybe we should look at that.'

Robert interrupted before Craig could say anymore. 'I don't know how we can do that with the route we have planned.'

'I'm sure we can come up with something,' Craig said, not looking at Robert as he spoke.

Jen looked from Robert to Craig, then to John. 'You must get a lot of tourists through here,' she said.

John nodded. 'We do. And I always make time for a chat and to ask where they're from.'

Andie had only been half listening to the conversation. Listening to John talk about his wife passing away had unsettled her. Or, more specifically, it was the thoughts of what it must be like for him now. From one day being part of a couple to the next where he had to navigate life on his own, at least for now. How different would it be from navigating as a couple to navigating alone?

'It's getting late,' Andie said. 'We should probably head off.'

As they walked back along the esplanade, Andie looked at the moonlight glistening on the water. It looked calm and peaceful, and she wished she felt the same.

Beside her, Jen was also gazing at the water, wishing their surroundings could change her disposition.

Neither of them said anything. So neither of them knew the other also had a myriad of thoughts swirling through her mind.

'Too early for bed,' Robert said when they got back. 'How about we play cards?'

Andie could see that Craig was tired, but he could never turn down a game of cards.

'I'll get our table,' he said. 'And our cards are in the cupboard just inside the door.'

'I'll get some wine,' Robert said as he hurried off to their caravan.

Jen turned to look at Andie. 'You know we couldn't leave without packing several bottles of wine.'

Andie smiled. 'Yes, I know Robert likes his wine.'

'Sometimes a bit too much,' Jen muttered under her breath.

Jen didn't say anymore, but she hoped that Robert would tone down his drinking on the trip. Without the stress of his job and with twelve months of adventures in front of them, she figured he'd have plenty of other things to do at the end of the day. But Craig had got up to grab the glasses at the same time, so maybe she was overreacting. And it was only the first day. They hadn't had a chance to settle into their new way of life. Something she hoped Robert would do sooner rather than later.

'Let's play poker,' Craig said after the table and chairs were set up.

Andie shook her head. Not poker. Craig would suggest they play for money, and that was something she wanted to avoid.

'How about something old school like Canasta?' she suggested instead.

Jen clapped her hands. 'It's been a while. I hope I remember how to play.'

'I'm sure it will come back to you,' Andie said.

'Maybe we should go over the rules before we start,' Robert said.

'I know them,' Craig said. 'I'll go through them.'

Robert poured them all a glass of wine while Craig summarised the rules. Andie looked at him, but he said nothing about swapping the wine for a beer. Instead, he took a sip. Andie looked at the bottle. She knew it was an expensive one. So did Craig. When they were ready to start, he dealt the cards.

'A few hands only,' Jen said. 'I don't want to be tired tomorrow. I want to get the most out of our day trip.'

Andie nodded in agreement. 'Me too.'

'We can play for a while yet,' Robert said. 'It's not that late.'

'I'm sticking to a few hands only,' Jen said.

Craig looked up from his cards. 'What if you're winning?'

'Doesn't matter.'

True to her word, an hour later, Jen went to bed. Andie went soon after. Before turning in, she opened her laptop and added a mention of Malcolm and John on the blog, the first people they'd met on the trip. She didn't mention John's wife. That was too personal. Neither of them was awake when their husbands finally came to bed. And both of them had trouble waking them the next day.

'No sympathy,' Jen said to Robert the following morning. 'You shouldn't have stayed up so late or drank so much.'

'But I was only one game away from winning.'

Jen sighed. Why did he always have to be so competitive? Especially with Craig. They never used to be like that. When they first met, Robert and Craig spent a lot of time together. But something happened, and she didn't know what. They just started spending less time together. She'd asked Robert, and all he said was they were both busy and didn't have as much time to catch up. Robert had changed though, ever since he started his new career. As much as she was proud of his achievements, she often missed the old Robert. Or Rob, as she used to call him.

Over in the other caravan, Craig was complaining about his headache.

'The tablets are in that drawer,' Andie said, pointing.

'Can you get them for me?'

Andie looked at him lying on the bed with his eyes closed. She got him the tablets and a glass of water.

'You better hope you feel all right before we get on that boat.'

'I will. And it was worth it. I was one game up.'

That explains everything Andie thought. 'Here's a coffee.'

'Bacon and eggs would be good.'

'Now you're pushing things too far.'

She watched as Craig walked out of the caravan fifteen minutes later, the bed unmade and the breakfast dishes still in the sink. If she'd asked him to do something about it, he would have. He also would have complained. But for once, she'd like him to do something without being asked. To notice what needed to be done. To notice that he left her to clean up. To notice her. Like Jen, she was counting on this trip for more than just an adventure.

'Morning,' Jen said as she stood in the doorway of their caravan. 'I see Craig is in the same state as Robert.'

Andie nodded.

'Oh well. At least we'll have a good day. Let's go.'

'But I haven't had breakfast,' Robert groaned from behind Jen.

'You'll have to get something on the boat,' she replied. 'If we don't leave now, we'll miss it.'

From the moment Andie stepped on board, she felt content. It was a beautiful day, and the sun was glistening on the bright blue water. She and Jen leaned over the railing as the guys went inside, searching for food.

'Do you remember the day we met?' Jen said.

Andie nodded. 'We were in line at the tuckshop.'

Jen smiled. 'We both wanted a pie for lunch.'

'Tuckshop was the once-a-week treat for both of us.' Andie smiled as memories from her childhood came flooding back.

'It was so exciting being able to order what we wanted instead of eating whatever was packed for our lunches,' Jen said. 'Now it's the opposite. I buy lunch almost every day. I just don't have time in the morning to make anything.'

Andie made her lunches most days. It was cheaper than buying something from any of the lunch places that were near her school.

'How long is the boat trip?' Andie asked, wanting to change the subject. 'I don't remember. It's been too long since the last time I did it.'

'It's about thirty minutes. Robert checked the website last night before dinner.'

Andie laughed. 'Of course he did.'

'I wonder if they've found anything suitably greasy or deep fried?'

Jen got the answer to her question a minute later when Robert and Craig both walked out on the deck, each with a sausage roll, a dim sim, a packet of barbeque chips and a Coke to wash it all down.

'Are you trying to clog up your arteries as well as cure your hangover?' Jen said.

'We'll be right as rain after this,' Craig said.

Jen stared at the food again. 'Barbeque chips are an interesting addition.'

'I always have barbeque chips if I'm not feeling well on a boat,' Craig said. 'They make me feel better.'

Jen laughed. 'And I'm sure there's a scientific explanation to back that up.'

They were spared Craig's further explanation by the sound of the horn announcing their departure. As they moved away from the dock, two children waved, and Andie waved back. She couldn't remember the last time something so simple delighted her so much.

As the boat picked up speed, Andie and Jen moved to the front of the boat. It was windy, and the saltwater spray left them with damp, knotted hair. But neither of them moved. As the boat came closer to the island, Andie could see their transport waiting—a large four-wheel drive bus that would take them from the dock to the sand tracks where their tour would begin.

As the bus went through the gate that separated the sand from the bitumen, it started to tilt to one side, and the ground became alarmingly close. Andie decided to look up, not down, and for as far as she could see, the track was uneven. She pulled her seat belt tighter as they drove over the bumps and dips. Eventually, the track evened out, and she turned her attention to the scenery, which, surprisingly, didn't look familiar. When she thought about it though, it probably shouldn't. It was a long time ago, the last time she'd been here—another life and with another person.

Their first stop was Lake Mackenzie, with its pure, white sandy shores and azure water, which changed to an inky blue in the centre. Andie had her swimmers on, but she only went in as far as her ankles, the icy temperature stopping her from going any further. But it hadn't stopped a group of parents and children from swimming, and it hadn't stopped Craig and Rob. Robert, she reminded herself. Craig had been the first to go in, with Robert following a minute later. Andie could tell they were both cold, but neither of them was going to admit that. Jen stood on the shore with Andie.

'I wonder how long they'll last.'

Andie shrugged. 'Neither will want to get out first.'

'They'll probably wait until we need to leave.'

Jen's prediction came true, and it was only when their tour guide announced that it was time to go that they got out.

Back on the bus, their tour guide turned around and picked up his microphone.

'For those who don't know, Fraser Island is the largest sand island in the world. It's over 123 kilometres long and, at its widest part, 22 kilometres across, covering an area of 184,000 hectares. The island also has World Heritage listing along with other places in Australia, such as Uluru, Kakadu and the Great Barrier Reef. Fraser Island is also home to rainforests, sand dunes, and beautiful lakes.'

Andie listened and took notes as he spoke so she could add them to the blog later. When she was done, she looked out the window and standing just off the track was a dingo. Andie pointed it out to Craig.

'That's close enough for me.'

Robert turned to see what they were looking at. 'I agree with Craig. In fact, I'd prefer to only see them behind a tall fence.'

'But this is their home,' Jen said. 'They shouldn't be locked up. That's cruel.'

'I'd rather them locked up than us getting attacked,' Robert said.

'If you leave them alone, they'll leave you alone,' Jen said.

'That's good because I don't want to go anywhere near them,' Robert said.

Jen turned to look at him. 'When did you become so anti-animal?'

Robert shook his head. 'I'm not. But you know I prefer concrete to nature.'

'Yes, but you wanted to come on this trip, and we'll have more experiences with nature than with concrete.'

Robert shrugged. 'If I don't want to do some of the nature experiences, I'm sure you can go with Craig and Andie.'

Andie turned around. The look on Jen's face said all she needed to know. 'You're welcome to go anywhere we go, Jen. And there'll be times when we'll do something – just the two of us.'

Craig was too busy listening to the tour guide to notice anything that had been said.

When the bus arrived at their next destination, Central Station, Andie wandered away from the others for a few minutes, taking in the beauty surrounding her. So picturesque and tranquil. And then, for the second time that day, she saw a dingo. It was on the opposite side of a creek, about thirty metres from where she was standing. She wasn't worried that it was there. In fact, it only added to the scene around her, making it more complete. On the other hand, Craig and Robert, who'd caught up with her, were turning their heads from side to side, seeing if there were any big sticks they could quickly grab if the dingo decided to spring across the water. But it didn't. It just stared at them for a while, then turned around and disappeared into the rainforest.

When Jen came back, she was annoyed that she'd missed seeing it.

'Well, you're the one who left to go to the toilet,' Robert said.

'What was I supposed to do? I had to go.'

Craig turned to look at her. 'You didn't miss much. And you saw one from the bus.'

'But I wanted to see one close up.'

'Why?' Robert said. 'They're dangerous. You don't need to do that.'

'We were fine,' Andie said, interrupting the direction of the conversation. 'It stayed away from us.'

Then she turned to Jen. 'I'm sure there'll be plenty of other opportunities on the trip to see one.'

Andie watched as Jen, after glaring at Robert, walked away. She thought about following her, but she sensed that Jen needed a minute or two on her own. Instead, Andie reflected on how she'd felt being that close to a dingo and not being afraid. Maybe she was braver than she thought.

From a distance, Jen looked back at Robert. Why did he have to do things like that? She couldn't decide if she was furious or upset. Or maybe both. Over the years, he'd been dismissive of her feelings at various times. But up until recently, she'd always called him out on it. The energy to do that had faded like many of her feelings.

She waited until Robert started moving on, and then she walked closer to the creek, hoping the dingo would make another appearance. But as she stood and watched, the bush remained still. She continued to wait until the others in their group were almost out of sight before turning to go.

By the time they got back to the dock late that afternoon, Jen had let her annoyance at Robert fade. That was until Robert and Craig spotted the bar by the water.

'We've got time for one before we have to get back on the boat,' Robert said. 'Maybe two.'

'We could just go for a walk,' Jen said.

Robert shook his head. 'We've been out and about all day. I want to relax for a bit.'

Craig nodded. 'Me too. You two can go for a walk if you want.'

Andie turned to Jen. 'I'm a bit tired after our all-day adventure. I wouldn't mind just sitting by the water if that's all right with you.'

For a moment, Andie thought Jen would say no. But the moment passed, and she nodded.

.

As they waited for their drinks, Andie turned to Craig and asked what he thought of the island.

'It's great. You were right. I should have visited years ago.'

Robert nodded. 'That's what I said to him yesterday.'

A look crossed Craig's face, brief enough that only Andie noticed.

'Will we be able to see the sunset before we need to get on the boat?' she said.

Robert nodded. 'The boat leaves just before the sun goes down completely.'

It didn't take Craig and Robert long to go through their first drink and discuss getting another.

'How about we go and sit on the sand?' Jen said.

Robert shook his head. 'Why would we do that when we've got the same view here and comfortable chairs to sit on.'

The view really was beautiful, looking out over the passage and back to the mainland. Jen could see the colours changing as the sun started its downward journey. When she wasn't taking photos, she kept her eyes on it, watching the golden rays spread across the water. The sky became pink, then started to go darker. Just before the sun disappeared completely, the boat pulled up at the dock, and they left their table to walk down to the jetty. It was dark when they got back to the mainland, and she had to drive them back to the caravan park. Robert had decided to have one more drink on the boat.

'Great second day of our trip,' Robert said, back at the caravan park, a wine glass in his hand.

Craig nodded as he sipped his beer. 'Totally agree.'

Neither Andie nor Jen was drinking. And they didn't think their husbands should be either.

'What are we doing for dinner tonight?' Craig said.

Andie looked over at him. 'Always thinking of your stomach.'

'I'm hungry. We did a lot today and I haven't eaten since lunch.'

'We could stay here tonight. We've got plenty of food, and there's a BBQ just over there.'

'Sounds good to me.'

'Are you sure you don't want to try another restaurant?' Robert said, interrupting Andie and Craig. 'We might never come back to Hervey Bay, and we can BBQ anytime.'

'You'll be able to say that everywhere we go,' Jen said. 'I'm happy to have a BBQ here.'

'I guess I'm outvoted. BBQ it is.'

'Great,' Jen said as she turned to Andie, smiling.

Andie smiled back at her. It wouldn't occur to Robert to consider the differences in their finances.

Not long afterwards, while Craig and Robert stood around the BBQ, debating the best way to cook the meat, Andie added the next blog entry.

Fraser Island

We had a wonderful day on Fraser Island. It's such a beautiful place. After spending time at Lake McKenzie, we continued to Central Station, where we came across rainforest trees growing in sand! And the water flowing through the creek was so clear, it looked like there was no water at all!

Andie pondered whether to mention the dingo sighting but decided not to. Best not to remind Jen about what she'd missed. And what she would have liked to miss – Robert's reaction.

After that, we headed east, coming out on the surf side of the island. We spent the rest of the tour on that side, visiting the Champagne Pools, Indian Head, the Mehano Shipwreck and Eli Creek. We crammed in a lot during the day, and we were tired by the end, but it was worth it. Every place we visited was stunning, with such natural beauty and places you won't find anywhere else in the world. We ended by watching the sunset back on the western side of the island while waiting for the boat. Jen's photos of the sunset will show you how beautiful a sight it was. As will all the pictures she took of the places we visited.

Before clicking save, Andie added the information the tour guide had told them about the island, along with Jen's photos and some info Jen read from her phone as Andie typed. Second entry done, she thought to herself as she closed her laptop.

The next morning, they packed up the caravans and headed north. Their destination was Emu Park. They'd only been driving for just under three hours when Jen called.

'We have to stop,' she said. 'There's a crab on the roof of a service station.'

What on earth is she talking about Andie wondered. And then she saw it—a giant, fibreglass crab atop the building next to the petrol pumps. Jen got out of their car and took a photo.

'Didn't expect to see that,' Craig said. 'We're not near the ocean.'

Both couples walked into the service station and through to the Big Crab restaurant at the back. There were a lot of crab sandwiches and the usual hamburgers, pies, and crumbed sausages that you find in similar types of places.

'We have to try one,' Jen said.

'You think they'll be all right?' Robert said. 'It's seafood, and we're in a service station.'

'Where's your sense of adventure?'

'Inside me, where I'd like the contents of my stomach to stay.'

'It'll be fine,' Craig said, chiming in. 'I'll have one.'

Robert looked at Jen and then at Craig and Andie before turning to the woman behind the counter. 'Four crab sandwiches, please.'

Even as he ordered, he still didn't look convinced, but his first bite changed his opinion. 'It's delicious and unexpected. I wonder how many places like this we'll come across on the trip.'

Andie smiled to herself at seeing a hint of the old Robert. Jen looked happy about it too. Craig was too busy eating to notice Robert or that Jen wouldn't take any money from Andie for the sandwiches.

Fifteen minutes later, food eaten, coffees drunk, and bathroom trips completed, they were back on the road. They didn't get very far though. Only another eighty-six kilometres.

'Fishing stop,' Craig said, something he'd spoken about with Robert but not with her or Jen.

Andie sighed. Day three, and they were fishing already. There were more hours ahead of them to get to that day's destination, and she would have liked to get there. But she realised that stopping at unexpected places would happen throughout the trip and that those stops might lead to something remarkable.

Through her car window, Andie could see Jen with her camera lifted. 'Second photo of the day,' she called out.

Jen nodded. 'I don't think we need to add a fishing stop to the blog, but a few months from now, I might not remember we called in at the Calliope River.'

Neither Jen nor Andie wanted to fish, so they sat on the bank and left the guys to it. Fishing was one of the few things Robert continued to do after his career change. Although, it was something he now did with people he met through his work. People who could help further his career. He and Craig used to go regularly, but those fishing trips began to dwindle once Robert got his big promotion.

'So, will this be dinner?' Jen hollered out.

Robert and Craig turned around to look at her, but neither said anything.

Andie smiled. 'If they don't catch anything, I'm sure one of them will say that the fish aren't biting.'

'Or we got here too late in the day, and the best fishing is first thing in the morning.'

'They seem to be having fun though.'

And getting along, Andie thought.

'So how do you think you and Craig will go spending every day of the next twelve months together?'

Andie paused before answering. 'Ok, I think. We've never actually spent three hundred and sixty-five days together in such close quarters.'

Jen nodded. 'The caravan could be an issue. It's not a big space, and Robert re-organised the inside three times before we left. As well as doing it again in Hervey Bay.'

Andie laughed. 'That doesn't surprise me. I don't know how you put up with it.'

Jen shook her head. 'Sometimes I have no idea.'

Andie turned to look at her. 'How do you think the two of you will go for the next twelve months?'

'I think it will be easier for me than for Rob.'

'Good thing he's out of earshot.'

Jen laughed. 'Yes, but he was Rob when I met him, and I still say it sometimes.'

'I sometimes forget too.'

'It's only since he got his promotion six years ago that he's been insisting on Robert.'

'That's also around the time you got your promotion.'

'Yes, and while we love our careers, I'm looking forward to spending time together and exploring new places.'

Andie smiled. 'Especially the ones that are in cities.'

'Rob used to love going to out-of-the-way places. I'm sure it won't take him long to enjoy them again.'

Something in her voice made Andie wonder if it would take longer than Jen would admit.

They continued talking and taking in the surrounding scenery until the guys were done fishing. No one mentioned that no fish had been caught.

Back in the cars, Jen stared out the window as Robert drove but couldn't focus on anything. They'd only just left, so she should have been happy about everything they were going to experience. The places they'd visit, the people they would meet. And the opportunity to take time out of their busy lives and enjoy the change.

But in the back of her mind, she was wondering if she was putting too much pressure on the trip and what she hoped it would do rather than enjoying it for what it was. And that while they were away, she'd see glimpses of the old Robert, the one she had fallen in love with all those years ago. Even a brief glimpse to start with would do, then hopefully another and another after that.

It wasn't something she could talk to Andie about. And it certainly wasn't something she could talk to Robert about.

He'd say she was overthinking things, and there was nothing wrong. But as much as she'd like to believe that, she couldn't.

Chapter Three

Rockhampton and Emu Park

It feels like we've done so much already, yet we've only just started. It's exciting to think about what's to come. We're continuing our journey north, the highway stretching in front of us, long and straight, with nothing much to look at. Except for an austere landscape, as far as I can see. Dusty brown, and what grass survives, looks brittle, a mix of yellow and brown. Some trees scattered across the landscape have leaves, others just bare branches. I wonder when the last rains fell. It's farming land, and cattle, all through the region. How do the farmers continue in this environment?

Andie looked down at what she'd just written as well as the other entries. Would anyone be interested in reading this? While she pondered the question, she stared out the window and started counting the carriages on the coal train that snaked along the edge of the highway. She counted to twenty-seven before she got distracted and lost count. She checked the map when they got to Mount Larcom. Not far to go. Only 75 kilometres.

It was just under an hour later when Andie's phone beeped.

There's a bull on the roundabout! Jen's text read.

Not a real one, I hope! Andie replied

No. You'll see in a minute.

As Jen and Robert entered the roundabout and Andie's view was no longer obstructed by their caravan, she could indeed see a statue of a bull, along with a sign that said, *Welcome to Rockhampton, The Beef Capital of Australia.*

'Look at that,' Andie said, pointing it out to Craig.

He laughed. 'One of the guys on a building site told me about that. He said people keep stealing the balls off the statue.'

'Trust you to find that amusing.'

Even as she said it, she couldn't help looking, and the statue was definitely not complete.

Once they'd exited the roundabout, more houses came into view, and before long, they were in the middle of the city. They kept driving until they saw the sign for the bridge that they needed to cross the Fitzroy River. Andie's phone beeped again.

Look at the pub on the right. Lovely building.

Yes. Craig wants to stop and have a look.

Robert wants to keep driving and set up. Maybe we could come back tomorrow.

Good idea. Let's do that.

She ignored Craig's grumbling after she sent the text.

As they drove across the river, Andie noticed how high and how fast it was moving. It must have rained a lot recently in the river's catchment. She couldn't help thinking of the contrast to the dry landscape they'd seen just over an hour out of town. At the end of the bridge, they saw a sign that said Yeppoon, so they turned right. They weren't going that far, but it was the same road to their destination.

'This is a lovely spot,' Jen said when they'd arrived. 'And it looks like a quiet place to relax. Just what I need. Working and packing last week was exhausting.'

Craig turned to look at her. 'Why didn't you take the week off?'

Jen shook her head. 'I couldn't. I had a meeting in Sydney I had to fly down for on Wednesday and a presentation to the board on Friday.'

'Couldn't someone else do it?'

'No, they couldn't.'

'Here's a beer, Craig,' Andie said, handing him the bottle and interrupting the conversation. 'How about we set the caravan up?'

Jen looked at Craig as he started setting up. His viewpoint wasn't that different to a lot of people. Very few understood the demands of her job. And how much pride she had in her achievements. It had taken a lot from her, though. Chasing promotions had taken time. Time away from other things she could have done. New hobbies, maybe. Learning a new skill. Spending time with Robert.

The last one was a two-way street, though. He'd spent his time regularly chasing better job opportunities, meaning the time available to spend with her had become less and less.

'Let's have a look around Emu Park,' Robert said once they were done. 'I think we can walk through this park.'

'Good idea,' Jen said. She was happy to move away from the caravan. As well as setting up, Robert had again rearranged a few of her things into what he called a more logical order. Again. As tempted as she was to move items back, she couldn't be bothered having to deal with his reaction if she did. She'd learned long ago just to let some things go. Not everything though.

As they headed into the park, Jen consulted her phone. 'Bell Park was built between the 1910s and 1940s and was heritage listed in 2003. Apparently, there used to be lots of large company picnics here in the 1940s.'

Andie gazed at her surroundings - the mature pine trees dotted along the eastern side of the park, the open grassed areas highlighted in a mixture of sun and shade, pausing when she observed a timber structure. 'Does it say what that is?'

Jen glanced up to see where Andie was pointing, then scrolled through the website she'd found. 'The timber tower is thought to be a judge's box or starters box because it overlooks a large, flat expanse of grass, said to be a runners track.'

'That's interesting. I'll add those details to the blog. Make sure you get some photos.'

Jen laughed. 'As if you need to ask.'

Andie laughed too. She doubted she would have to ask Jen any time during the trip to take photos.

Craig, who hadn't paid attention to what Jen had said, was looking in the opposite direction. 'Where does that path go?'

They headed to where he had been looking and caught a glimpse of the ocean.

'Let's see what's there,' Jen said, getting out her phone again to check the map.

'Fisherman's Beach,' she said as they walked off the end of the path and onto a long stretch of sand.

'With a name like that, we'll have to get the rods out,' Craig said. 'Maybe even you can have a go, Andie.'

'We'll see.'

'I'll have a go if you will,' Jen said.

'All right. As long as I don't have to put the worms on the hook.'

'I wonder which island that is?' Craig said, pointing straight in front of them.

Robert answered before anyone else had a chance to. 'That's Great Keppel. We should go over and have a look.'

'Another island,' Craig said. 'That's two in three days.'

Andie pointed in front of them. 'It's just over there. We may as well go.'

Craig shook his head. He'd already had enough of Robert dictating where they should and shouldn't go. And it was only early in the trip.

'Come on,' Jen said. 'Let's keep walking.'

They continued on, climbing the hill upon which the Singing Ship sat, then down the other side, around a bend and then on to another beach.

'There's a lifesaving shed,' Andie said. 'This must be the swimming beach.'

Jen consulted her phone. 'Pine Beach, named for all the pine trees in the park behind us.'

Andie looked out at the ocean. 'I wouldn't mind going for a swim tomorrow.'

Craig nodded. 'That sounds good. And don't forget the fishing.'

Jen turned to look at Craig. 'What about going into Rockhampton?'

'We can do that the day after.'

'What about Great Keppel?'

Craig shrugged. 'We can't go to every island. Do we really need to go?'

Jen shook her head. 'I suppose not.'

'Right, now that's settled, why don't we cross the road and check out that pub,' Craig said, pleased that he'd nipped that suggestion in the bud.

Andie turned to look at him. 'You've just had a beer.'

Craig nodded. 'And now it's time for another one. Walking around town is thirsty work. I'm sure Robert would agree.'

Robert nodded. 'Absolutely. I wonder what sort of wine list they've got?'

'Only one way to find out,' Craig said, a grin on his face, happy that Robert was doing what he wanted.

They crossed the road, walked inside and ordered.

'Look,' Jen said, pointing to a sign above the bar. 'We could come back for dinner. It's ten-dollar roast night.'

As they sat in the Pine Beach Hotel, Andie was again taken by the ocean views and the town's peacefulness, just as she had been in Hervey Bay. Outside, the road was quiet. During the time they sat there, Andie only saw five cars drive by. Across the street, she saw two older men walking through the park behind the beach. Shuffling was probably a more accurate description. They were deep in conversation, the kind you have with someone you've known for a long time. She wondered whether they'd always lived in the town or whether they'd retired there. She was thinking the former as they both had a weather-beaten look about them, one that comes from constant exposure to wind, sand, and salt water. What would it be like, living by the sea? Instead of wondering, she asked their waitress.

'I love it,' she said. 'I can't imagine living anywhere else. Walking on the beach every morning, swimming in the ocean whenever I want to, and the beautiful sea breezes in the afternoon. Why would I want to move?'

Andie thought about what the waitress had said for a long time after she'd left their table. It sounded like a wonderful way to live.

After they finished their drinks, they continued their walk around town and returned to the caravan park, only to find themselves back at the pub 90 minutes later. Before they'd left the pub, Robert suggested they stay. Jen had been the one to say no. She said she'd rather be outside after being in the car. Andie had seen a look pass between them, and Robert had said nothing further.

'Which roast are you going to have?' Jen asked.

'Lamb for me,' Andie said.

Robert nodded. 'I'm having the same.'

'I'll have the pork,' Craig said. 'Crackling is the best bit.'

'It's not very good for you,' Robert said, conscious that, out of the two of them, he was the one who could stand to lose some weight.

'If I only ate things that were good for me, I wouldn't enjoy eating very much,' Craig said. 'So, how do we work Bowen into the itinerary?'

Robert turned to look at him. 'We haven't decided to do that.'

'We talked about it in Hervey Bay,' Craig said.

'But we didn't decide anything.'

'It was recommended. I think we should do it.'

'And I don't think we'll have time,' Robert said, wishing Craig would stop pushing the point. He'd put a lot of time and effort into pulling together an itinerary that would enable them to get the most out of the trip. And he'd deliberately left Bowen off their planned route.

'We've got twelve months.'

'Which is all accounted for in our existing itinerary.'

'But there's no reason to be so rigid,' Craig said, his voice thick with frustration. 'I'm sure there'll be a lot of times we'll hear about a place we hadn't planned on going but would be worth seeing.'

Andie put down her wine glass. 'Enough, you two. I want to enjoy my dinner when it arrives.'

Craig turned to her. 'But we haven't sorted this out.'

Andie looked straight at him. 'We'll do that later.'

The conversation turned to what they would do the following day, apart from swimming and fishing, but only Andie and Jen spoke. The guys sat in silence. When they got back to the caravans, Andie and Jen sat up and continued the blog entry they'd started earlier. The guys sat up too, but the silence continued. As did the drinking.

Now, this is something you don't see every day. Andie added these words to Jen's photo of the bull on the roundabout. *We didn't spend any time in Rockhampton this afternoon as we wanted to get to our destination for the night and set up. But we'll go back into the city the day after tomorrow, and we'll let you know what we get up to.*

After our brief stop at the Calliope River, we drove to Emu Park.

Andy then added some notes from what Jen had come across earlier, along with a couple of photos. Then she added a new section.

On top of a hill, near the caravan park, is the Singing Ship. The monument commemorates Captain Cook and his exploration of the area in May 1770. It was built to represent the billowing sails, mast and rigging of the Endeavour. Inside it, there are concealed organ pipes that use the sea breezes to create music, hence its name. We were lucky enough to hear the music as we stood next to it, mesmerised by the view – a deep blue ocean and a spattering of islands laid out in front of us, all glittering in the sun. On the way back from dinner at the pub, Jen ran up the hill to take a photo of the Singing Ship at night, which you can see below.

As Andy was typing, a thought floated through her mind. Fleeting, but there, nonetheless. A thought where she wished they'd lived somewhere she could walk by the ocean any time she wanted.

The next day they got up early, and Andie went for a walk along Fisherman's Beach. It was a long beach, and she decided to walk from one end to the other. Craig and Robert were already fishing, and Jen had decided to explore the park again. She hadn't walked very far when she heard a shout from Robert. He must have caught a fish. But she didn't turn around to check. She was too focused on the sun shining on the water, the soft sand under her feet and the ocean breeze against her skin. It was the perfect spot to think about Craig. She'd done a lot of that in the past few months.

Forty-five wasn't twenty-five. A lot had changed in the past twenty years since their wedding. Thinking back, she could picture the day she'd been visiting a friend when she and Craig had been apart. She happened to glance over the fence, and in the yard next door, builders were putting up a house frame. One of those builders had been Craig. He waved when he saw her, and she waved back. Then they started talking. Before she knew it, they were back together, then living together, and then marriage followed. And now here she was, all these years later, still with Craig.

Andie kept looking at the ocean, hoping it would distract her. But even wondering what cargo was on the passing ships didn't take her mind off the thoughts that had become more frequent.

The doubts had started to creep in after what turned out to be their last attempt at IVF. They'd tried five times with no success. Andie had thought about trying again, but the emotional toll was too much. She still felt it, but Craig didn't want to talk about it anymore. And she couldn't talk to Jen because she and Robert had never wanted children. Craig was supportive during the first attempt, but with each new attempt, he became less so. The further he withdrew, the more Andie wondered if this was who she wanted to spend the rest of her life with. Being married and still feeling alone—it hadn't occurred to her that it was possible, but that's how she felt.

On her way back, she turned her thoughts to other things. She needed the tears to dry before she got back to the caravan.

In the park, Jen would have been surprised to know that her thoughts weren't far from what Andie was thinking. She couldn't recall the exact moment she began to feel unhappy. Or that what she had wasn't enough anymore. If she and Robert were going to stay together for the rest of their lives, then she needed more. And she hoped this trip would bring the more she craved. Thankfully, there was plenty of time for it, as they'd only just hit the road. She couldn't expect anything to change already. So why did she?

Unlike Andie and Craig, Jen and Robert had met in their twenties. They'd both been in other relationships, had done some travel, and had embarked on their careers. When they met, at a mutual friend's party, neither was looking for a relationship. But they found themselves talking for the rest of the night and then agreeing to meet for a coffee a few days later. The coffee turned into a walk, then into lunch, then into an exhibition at an art gallery, and then into dinner. By the time they said goodbye, many hours after they'd originally planned, they both concluded that they should rethink their individual decisions to not be in a relationship and see where things might go.

Where things went, after a few years, was marriage. Andie had been her Matron of Honour, and Craig had been one of the groomsmen. Jen had been pleased that Robert and Craig got along from the moment they'd been introduced. She loved the idea of the four of them doing things together. And they had, for a long time. Until she and Robert had decided to make something more of their careers. While she had been able to balance that new focus with everything else in her life, including her friendships, Robert wasn't quite as good. They still did things together, but only if she or Andie organised it. Along with everything else Jen wanted from this trip, she would love to see Robert and Craig be the friends they once were. Depending on what happened over the next twelve months, Robert might need someone in his corner.

'This is the first major regional city on our trip,' Jen said after she parked the car in Rockhampton. 'This is exciting.'

There had been a long discussion before they'd left about whose car to take, with Craig and Robert volunteering to drive. Neither one wanted to give in, and eventually, Jen put a stop to the conversation by saying she'd drive.

'What's first up?' Craig asked. 'And when are we going to the pub?'

'What's with you and this pub?' Robert asked. 'It's not like you've been there before.'

'No, no. It's just a great old building, and I'd like to see what the inside looks like.'

Andie turned to look at him. 'I've never known you to be interested in the architecture of old buildings. You're usually only interested in new buildings and, even then, just the ones you've built.'

'I've been interested before.'

Andie continued looking at him, trying to think when that had been, but she couldn't pinpoint any particular instance. 'We'll go later. Let's do some sightseeing first.'

A few hours later, Craig finally got his wish.

'It's a nice pub,' Robert said. 'But I don't know if it's worth getting as excited about as you've been.'

Craig looked around him to make sure Andie and Jen weren't in earshot. 'I've been here before.'

Robert looked at him. 'And?'

'Before Andie and I got back together.'

'I see. I think I know where this is going.'

'I was in Rockhampton for work and came here one night and met someone.'

'Must have been a memorable someone.'

Craig smiled. 'She was.'

'So why do you want to remember that now?'

Craig shrugged. 'I don't know. I just do.'

After eating, Robert got up to go to the bathroom. And on the way back, he paid the bill for all of them.

'You didn't have to do that,' Andie said.

'I know. But I thought it would be a nice gesture.'

'A nice gesture,' Craig mimicked once Robert and Jen were out of earshot. 'Showing off is more like it. Reminding us about the money they have.'

'Let it go,' Andie sighed.

She wasn't in the mood for that type of conversation. And she'd also noticed the look on Jen's face. Andie knew her well enough to know the frown wasn't because Robert had paid. It was because it wouldn't have occurred to him that maybe the gesture would be taken the wrong way. Which it had been. By Craig. Although Andie couldn't be absolutely sure, she felt that Robert had been showing off. Just a bit.

Later that afternoon, in the car on the way back to the caravans, Andie added to the existing blog entry.

Rockhampton is the fourth largest city in Queensland, the first three being in the southeast of the state. We spent the morning wandering around, looking at some of the older historic buildings. Then, continuing with that theme, we headed to the Heritage Village. A township museum that showcases aspects of the district over a one-hundred-year period between 1850 and 1950. It was interesting to see depictions of times gone by, and we all enjoyed it.

The last sentence was a white lie. Craig and Robert hadn't been interested, but Andie didn't include that. She and Jen had enjoyed the look back in time, interested in how people lived back then. And how happy they were, Andy thought to herself.

After lunch, we headed out to the Capricorn Caves, a
series of limestone caves that we explored, gazing at their
structure and listening to the acoustics.

Craig had hollered to test the acoustics, but Andy didn't
add that to the blog. Nor did she add that she'd told him to shut
up. He'd been acting strangely since lunch, and even though
she'd asked him about it, he kept silent.

When they got back to the caravan park, she added Jen's
photos then closed the laptop. She'd had enough of staring at a
screen. Instead, she walked down to the beach by herself and
stared at the ocean. And also at the locals she saw walking along
the water's edge. Every one of them looked relaxed and happy.

Several hours later, after dinner and after cards, and after
Craig had too many beers, Andie tried to put him to bed.

'It's too early.'

'No, it's not. Come on.'

'Andie's right,' Robert said, who for once had drunk less
than Craig. 'Let's all go to bed.'

'Don't you want to hear more of my story, mate?'

'What's he talking about?' Andie said.

'Nothing,' Robert said.

'It's not nothing. I told you about my night at the Criterion and what happened afterwards.'

'Shut up, Craig. Go to bed.'

Jen got up from her chair. 'I'll help put him to bed.'

Craig shook his head. 'Don't want to go.'

Andie sighed. 'Well, you are.'

'Don't you want to hear my story?'

Robert shook his head. 'No, Andie doesn't want to hear it either. Let's go.'

All three of them got Craig in the caravan, where he fell asleep as soon as he was on the bed.

An hour later, Andie was still awake. Not because she wasn't tired but because Craig was snoring like a freight train. It was so loud that she considered sleeping outside before deciding it probably wasn't safe. Eventually, she got up and found some earplugs. But even with those pushed firmly in her ears, she could still hear him. She got up again and found her beanie. It was too warm to wear, but she figured it had to help as she pulled it down over her ears. But even the extra layer didn't drown out the noise. She got up again, took off the beanie, took out the earplugs and took a sleeping tablet as a last resort. It was the only way she'd get any sleep.

The next morning, she asked Craig what he'd been going on about. He mumbled something, but she couldn't understand him, and then he rolled back over, putting the pillow over his head. Andie decided to leave him and went outside. She asked Robert instead.

'Nothing important.'

'You wouldn't tell me last night either.'

'It's not worth telling.'

'I'll decide that after you tell me.'

Jen got up from her chair and walked over. 'Now I'm intrigued as well. What's the story?'

Robert waited a moment before replying. 'It was just about a girl he met at that pub years ago when he and Andie weren't together.'

'Why would he be talking about that now?' Jen asked.

Robert shrugged. 'No idea. Anyway, it doesn't matter. Let's start packing up. Andie, I think you might be driving this morning.'

'I'll drive too,' Jen said. 'Ladies convoy today.'

Andie started packing up and eventually got Craig out of bed. But she couldn't stop thinking about what Jen had said. Why was Craig thinking about that now?

Chapter Four

By mid-morning, they were heading off to Seaforth, that day's destination.

'Why were you talking about a woman you met years ago?' Andie said.

In the passenger seat, Craig rubbed his eyes. 'What?'

'To Robert at the pub.'

Craig shrugged. 'Don't know. Just remembered it.'

'Apparently, you remembered it very well.'

'What's it matter now? It was a long time ago.'

'Yes, but you're thinking about it now.'

'I don't want to talk about it anymore.' Craig said, not wanting to tell Andie the real reason. That lately, he'd been feeling his age and wondering where the last twenty-five years had gone.

From then on, they drove in silence—Craig staring out the window and Andie staring straight ahead, both hands gripping the steering wheel. She thought back to her walk on the beach. Maybe they had grown too far apart.

The closer they got to Mackay, their turn-off point to Seaforth, cane fields came into view, lining both sides of the road. Andie glanced at them as she drove. It was a pity none were burning. She'd seen cane fields burn once before, many years ago, on a trip with Craig. They'd gone to a wedding, one of Craig's cousins. The wedding had been held at the family property, and to get there, they'd driven through small country towns, along back roads and through cane fields. They'd almost reached their destination when Andie saw the flames. She'd asked Craig to pull over, and they'd sat and watched for a few minutes. Thinking about it now, she was taken by the idea that when the fire had burnt out, all that remained was what was important. What wasn't needed no longer existed.

In the other car, things weren't much better.

'You can go a lot faster,' Robert said. 'There's a line of cars behind us and a big gap in front between us and Craig and Andie.'

'It's not that big a gap, and I don't want to go any faster,' Jen replied.

'Why not?'

'This is the first time on a single-lane highway like this. I'm being cautious.'

'You practised highway driving before we left.'

'Yes, but that was double lanes. It felt like I had more space around me. This feels narrow.'

'That shouldn't matter.'

'But it does. Especially with all those trucks going by. I'm driving in a way I feel comfortable with.'

'Maybe we should swap, and I'll drive.'

'No, I'm happy driving.'

'I don't know that I am.'

'What's that supposed to mean?'

'I feel safer when I'm driving.'

'What are you talking about? My driving is perfectly safe.'

'I think mine is safer.'

'Oh, shut up. Are you suggesting you want to do all the driving from now on?'

'I could.'

'No, you couldn't. We're sharing the driving, and that's the end of it.'

'We'll talk about it again.'

'No, we won't. Now shut up so I can concentrate on the road.'

Jen kept the car at the same speed, seething. And trying not to let his words upset her. But no matter how hard she tried, she couldn't shake that feeling. Robert was supposed to be the one who was by her side, her partner, not the one she had to fight against.

As she continued to drive, he stayed silent. It was as if she was by herself. And she wondered how different things would be if she was in this car alone. Would she be enjoying the journey more? Would she be paying more attention to what was going on outside the car instead of what was going on inside it?

Trying to take her mind off Robert, she forced herself to take notice of what was happening all around her, not just what was happening on the road in front. Apart from the occasional farmhouse, there wasn't a lot out there, and she wondered what sort of person enjoyed living in this seclusion. Jen had grown up as a city girl and would always remain that way. She'd never had any inclination to move anywhere regional or rural. It just wasn't her. That was something she and Robert had in common. He was a city person too. The only difference was she was interested in seeing all the regional and rural areas they would go to. Robert, not so much.

With all her work travel, she spent plenty of time in the other capital cities, mainly the east coast ones, but she did occasionally get to the west. She loved the pace, variety and opportunities that were available. There was always something going on.

Out here, she imagined that people had to rely on those in close proximity to keep them entertained. If that were her, she'd become bored quite quickly, as Robert couldn't be counted on in a situation like that. Although, considering how she was feeling about him at the moment, she wouldn't have wanted to rely on him anyway.

She sighed as she stared at the sign on the side of the road, highlighting how many kilometres they had to go to get to their destination. This is not how she wanted the first few days of the trip to be. She'd been so excited before they left. And she was still excited now. But it was tinged with her feelings about Robert. And her annoyance at why things hadn't magically changed overnight. As if there was any chance that could be a reality and not just wishful thinking. If she wanted things to change, a lot needed to be done.

Late in the afternoon, they pulled up in Seaforth. They'd spent most of the day in Mackay, looking around the city and enjoying a picnic by the Pioneer River. Andie took plenty of notes, and Jen took plenty of photos. When they'd done everything in Mackay they'd wanted to, they moved on to their destination, where they'd found a free overnight camping spot with views of the ocean. Everyone liked the view. And Andie liked that it was free.

After they'd set up, Andie pulled out her laptop.

We've now travelled about 970 kilometres from home. Today we explored the 'sugar capital' of Australia, otherwise known as Mackay. We didn't know before we arrived that the Mackay region produces more than a third of the country's sugar. That would explain all the cane fields we saw as we drove.

'Do you want to go for a walk?' Jen said. 'I know you're writing the blog post, but there's not much time before the sun sets.'

Andie nodded and put her laptop away. Robert wanted to check something on the caravan, so he said he'd stay. Craig decided to do the same.

'I'm almost glad they didn't come,' Jen said as they reached the end of the path that led onto the sand. 'I've had enough of Robert today.'

'What's he done now?'

'Nothing about my driving was good enough.'

'You're a great driver.'

'Tell that to Robert.'

'He just doesn't like anyone else being in control.'

Jen nodded. 'I'm well aware of that. Sometimes I don't know if I want to put up with it anymore.'

'Do you really mean that?'

Jen sighed. 'Sometimes yes, sometimes no. I don't know what to think.'

They walked in silence for a while before Jen said she wanted to be alone.

Andie watched her walk off and wondered why she hadn't said anything. It might have helped Jen to know someone else was feeling the same way. But she really didn't have to wonder. She knew why she hadn't said anything. Even though the thoughts were becoming more frequent, if she said them aloud, they would become concrete.

It wasn't as if Robert had changed overnight, Jen thought to herself as she walked. Yes, he'd got worse in the last several years, ever since his work situation changed. But he'd always had aspects of the behaviour that was currently driving Jen crazy. The only difference was now it bothered her to the point where she didn't want to deal with it any longer. After so many years together, she was tired of it. At work, she never let anyone speak to her the way Robert did. So why did she let him get away with it?

Was it that she just didn't care anymore? Or was it something else? She hated the confusion she felt. She liked to be in control too. To know how everything was supposed to play out. Even this trip, where anything could happen day to day, there was a plan. Albeit, one that could be changed to incorporate whatever they needed it to, but a plan, nonetheless. A plan that Robert had overseen. One that, when anyone else tried to take over, caused him to dig his heels in and put everyone offside.

When she returned thirty minutes later, those thoughts were still in her mind as Jen pulled Andie aside.

'Sorry about that. It was a bit dramatic walking off.'

'Don't worry about it. Sometimes you need to be alone. Do you want to talk about it?

Jen sighed. 'It's just that Robert can be hard work sometimes.'

Andie didn't mean to smile, but she did.

A smile spread across Jen's face too. 'Yes, I'm aware I just stated the obvious.'

'He's not hard work all the time, is he?'

Jen sighed again. 'No, just most of the time.'

'Why is it bothering you now?'

'Because we're a bit older now, and I want my home life to be easier and less stressful. And because we'll be spending every day together for the next year without work providing a buffer for twelve hours a day.'

'I don't know how you manage those twelve-hour days plus all the travel. I would be exhausted.'

'It is exhausting at times, but I love it—the fast pace, the interesting challenges to work through. And I've made my way up the corporate ladder despite some men I work with trying to stop me. But I needed this break. We both did.'

Andie nodded. 'So did we.'

'So, what was Craig going on about back in Rockhampton and Emu Park?'

'Just being stupid. Reliving his youth. Who knows?'

'I know it's a cliché, but he's not having a mid-life crisis, is he?'

Andie shrugged. 'Maybe. That's crossed my mind a few times.'

Like after the night he went out with his workmates and came home drunk at five in the morning, Andie mused. Or the time he decided to try white water rafting, something he couldn't talk Andie into, no matter how much he tried. And not long before they left, he'd been talking about motorbike lessons. Maybe that's why he came up with the idea for the trip, Andie thought to herself. A mid-life crisis.

'Has he said anything like that?'

Andie shook her head. 'Not in those words. Maybe it's nothing. I want to forget about it for the moment.'

'Seems like both our husbands are causing us grief.'

Andie sighed. 'Lucky us.'

'At least we have a gorgeous setting.'

Andie gazed out at the ocean, the same ocean that had soothed her mind in Emu Park. But, this time, it didn't have the same effect.

The following day, they got up early for a bush walk through Cape Hillsborough National Park. From the minute they took their first steps, Andie found the peace she'd wanted the day before—the beautiful walking tracks, lined with trees, that brought them to the beach with its soft white sand where Andie dug her toes in, letting the feeling of being grounded wash over her. Robert, on the other hand, did nothing but complain.

'Why didn't you stay back at the caravan if you hate this so much?' Jen said.

'Because you would have complained if I didn't come.'

'It doesn't bother me if you're here or not.'

'Gee, thanks.'

'You know that's not what I meant. If you didn't want to do a bushwalk, you shouldn't have come.'

'But you would have spent the rest of the day saying I should have been there, that it was beautiful, that I didn't know what I missed out on.'

'No, I wouldn't.'

'Yes, you would.'

'Just stop talking and start walking.'

As Robert walked off, Jen watched in silence.

'Don't worry about it,' Craig said. 'He'll calm down.'

Andie turned to look at him, knowing he only said what he did because he was pleased that Robert was behaving badly. He looked at her and smiled, and kept walking.

'How have I put up with him for all these years?' Jen said as both husbands disappeared from view.

Andie sighed. 'You and me both.'

Jen turned to look at her.

'Not Robert. I was referring to Craig.'

Andie thought back to their wedding day. So much love and laughter. And so much excitement for their life ahead. A life they'd navigate together. And for a while, the excitement about the adventure they were on surrounded them and kept them happy. But eventually, it started to wan, and before Andie knew it, their nights consisted of watching TV in separate rooms. They rarely went out anymore, and when they did, it was usually with friends, not just the two of them. Weekends away were a thing of the past too. Maybe this trip would change that, and the spark would come back. But as much as she wished that would happen, she wasn't sure it would.

'I'm glad we spent the day here,' Jen said as they packed up that night, ready to head off early the following day. 'It was beautiful.'

Andie smiled. 'I assumed you liked it from the number of photos you took.'

'I didn't take that many. No more than I usually do. And besides, I wanted to get some shots of the sea, beach, and mountains for the blog.'

Andie hadn't written the entry yet. She wasn't sure she would. Yes, it was a beautiful spot, but she wasn't ready to be reminded of the conversations with Jen or Robert's behaviour. And Craig is oblivious to it all. And to how she was feeling.

The next morning, as they prepared to leave, Andie looked around her and wished their next stop was unobtrusive like this one. They were headed to a tourist mecca, and Andie wasn't in the frame of mind to be surrounded by a multitude of people. She kept those thoughts to herself as she hopped in the car and closed the door.

Chapter Five

When they arrived, it was worse than Andie imagined. Airlie Beach was swarming with tourists. And it wasn't even peak holiday season. Luckily Robert had rung ahead and booked them into a caravan park. They got the last two spots, and once they'd driven in, the no vacancy sign went up out the front. Everywhere Andie looked, people were coming out of restaurants, bars, shops and tourism booking offices, the number one attraction being a day or overnight trip to the islands. Andie sighed quietly to herself and wondered if she could just stay in the caravan. Jen couldn't wait to get started.

'This is going to be so much fun. How are we going to pick which island to go to?'

Robert laughed. 'Glad to see you so happy.'

Andie could tell by the look on Jen's face that she would have been happier if Robert had realised how much his criticism from the day before had upset her.

Ninety minutes later, Andie hadn't changed her mind about how she felt. While Jen was excitedly pointing at everything, Andie wanted to find a quiet café and order a cup of tea. She didn't actually drink tea, but it sounded more soothing than coffee. There were just too many people. Walking down the main street was like walking through the Queen Street Mall in Brisbane. No matter what part of the footpath she walked on, she was jostled by tourists, all speaking different languages, which, when combined, sounded like loud, overwhelming noise. It was too much.

'I can't wait to go to one of the islands,' Jen said. 'It's warm enough to swim. We could go snorkelling as well.'

'Let's do something spontaneous,' Andie said, speaking before thinking it through. 'We can leave the vans here and stay overnight.'

Hopefully, whichever island they chose would be less crowded. Quieter. More relaxed.

'But we've already paid for the van sites,' Robert said, his arms crossed.

Andie turned to look at him. He and Jen had all the money, yet he could still be such a scrooge. If anyone should be worried about the cost, it was her. But at that moment, with thoughts about her marriage swirling through her head, the thought of quieting her mind and getting herself back in balance was more of a priority than the budget. They'd just have to miss out on something later on. Which Craig would whinge about. But she'd worry about that when the time came.

Jen nodded. 'Let's do it. I want to do something spontaneous too.'

Although Andie could see that Robert wanted to say something, he wisely stayed silent. Jen had already started walking towards the closest tourist information centre and was almost through the door when the others caught up with her.

'There's a good deal going on Hamilton Island at the moment,' the woman behind the counter said.

Andie couldn't help but smile when she saw Robert's eyes light up at the mention of a good deal. That's all it took to change his perspective. And so, ten minutes later, they had two rooms and the ferry over and back booked.

As they stood on the deck later that day, the same feeling Andie had previously when she was out on the water started to return. And the boat's engines had only just roared into life.

'What stunning scenery,' Jen said as the boat began to pull out of Shute Harbour. 'Which island is Hamilton?'

Andie pointed in the direction of the one they were heading to.

'I can see it already,' Jen said. 'It's not that far. I can't wait to get there.'

An hour and forty-five minutes later, Jen got her wish, and they disembarked.

'I don't think I'll be taking my sunglasses off while we're here,' Robert said as the sun blazed down.

Jen nodded. 'Isn't it great? I feel like it's summer again.'

Andy smiled. 'I think it's always summer here.'

A golf cart whizzed by as they picked up their bags from the wharf and headed towards the accommodation. Andie stopped for a moment, wondering what was going on. Then she remembered reading that golf carts were the main form of transport on the island. Something to note for the blog entry later. Craig had noticed too, and from the look on his face, Andie knew he couldn't wait to get behind the wheel of one and zip around the island. She sighed to herself. They were on a tropical island, and he was taken by something with a motor that wouldn't go anywhere near the beach or the ocean that surrounded them.

It didn't take long to check in, and as soon as Andie stepped into their room, the last doubt about suggesting they stay overnight faded from her mind. The view was breathtaking. Azure water, the sunlight reflecting on the tranquil surface, broken up by a scattering of islands as far as she could see. She stood for a few moments, mesmerised. She called Craig to come and look at the view, and when he didn't respond, she turned to see he wasn't there. She looked in the bedroom, but it was empty too. On the table near the door, where only a few minutes before, there had been two keys, now only one remained. She knew where he'd gone. And that he would have grabbed Robert on the way.

Andie debated whether or not to go and find him but decided to stay and look at the view for a while longer. She hadn't come to the island to sit in a bar. But she was annoyed. They were in a tropical paradise with a big room all to themselves. One that was more soundproof than the caravan, and he'd rather be at the bar. There was a time when he would have needed no encouragement to take advantage of an opportunity like this, but that had been a long time ago. Andie sighed. She didn't know what to do about that. And then there were the mentions of his one-night stand in Rockhampton all those years ago. She still hadn't found out why he'd brought that up. And she knew she wouldn't find out today. Craig would be on his second beer by the time she finally went to find him.

Half an hour later, she saw she'd been right. What she hadn't expected was that Robert was also on his second beer – wine, yes, but not beer.

'Thought I'd find you here,' Andie said.

Craig shrugged. 'Where else would we be?'

'Out enjoying the view.'

'There's a great view from here. And besides, you always go to the bar on a tropical island,' Craig said.

'Really?' Andie said. 'In that case, shouldn't you be drinking a cocktail with an umbrella in it?'

'You know I don't like cocktails,' Craig said.

Robert picked up his beer bottle. 'Maybe we could stick an umbrella in this.'

Craig laughed. 'That would look really stupid.'

Robert nodded. 'But it would keep Andie happy.'

'She's all right.'

Andie looked at him. 'Am I now?'

'Why wouldn't you be? Join us for a drink.'

Andie shook her head. 'I'm going for a walk to explore the place. Robert, do you know where Jen is?'

'She was tired, so she said she was going to lie down for a while.'

Andie had never heard of Jen resting during the day, so she decided to swing by her room and check.

She knocked on the door quietly in case Jen was asleep, but the door opened straight away.

'I only said that so Robert would go for a walk or something,' Jen said when Andie queried her. 'He won't stop going on about how we've paid for two lots of accommodation for tonight.'

'The caravan park wasn't expensive, and we got a great deal here,' Andie said while thinking that there was no reason for Robert to worry about the cost.

'I know.'

'Maybe that's why he's in the bar drinking beer with Craig.'

'Beer? He must be annoyed. Either that or they didn't have a very good wine selection.'

'I'm going for a walk to explore the island. Do you want to come?'

Jen nodded. 'Let me grab my hat and phone. We'll need some great photos that do the island justice for the blog.'

'It's stunning, isn't it?' Andie said as they stood at the edge of the sea, the water around their ankles so clear it was like glass.

Jen nodded. 'Let's walk along the beach. I want to feel the sand between my toes.'

They walked in silence, too busy taking in the scenery to chat. Not long after they'd started their circuit, they looked up and saw Craig and Robert still sitting in the same spot Andie had found them.

'Guess they're not moving anytime soon,' Jen said.

Andy nodded in agreement. She didn't agree with what they were doing, but they were adults, and it was their choice. She said as much to Jen, but from the look she gave Andie in return, it was clear she didn't agree.

'How much sightseeing did the two of you do today?' Jen asked later that afternoon.

'Plenty,' Robert said. 'We could see a lot from this vantage point.'

Jen looked from one to the other. 'Looking at the view from the bar is not the same as getting out and seeing the place.'

'It's an island,' Craig said. 'They're all the same.'

'What's all the same?' Andie said as she sat down at the table.

'These two were justifying why they spent the afternoon at the bar.'

'We don't have to justify anything,' Robert said. 'It's our trip too.'

Craig nodded. 'And this is how we wanted to spend the afternoon.'

Andie picked up the menu in front of her. 'Maybe we should order.'

As much as she tried to concentrate on the menu, she couldn't ignore that Craig and Robert had drunk too much. They were doing a good job of hiding it, but she could tell. From the look on Jen's face, she knew as well. At least Craig had stuck to beer. Robert had switched to wine at some point. Andie knew the only thing happening that night for her, or Jen, in their luxurious rooms would be trying to get some sleep next to drunk, snoring husbands.

Back in their room after dinner, Andie was leaning against the railing on the balcony. Down below, she could see the pool and the gardens encasing it, as well as the path Jen and Robert had taken to the building next door, illuminated against the night sky. Behind her, Craig was still snoring. The enthusiasm she'd had earlier for doing that day's blog entry had disappeared along with the hope that their location would inspire something romantic. Instead, she was standing alone in the middle of an island paradise. She turned away from the view and sighed. Enthusiasm or not, she may as well get the entry over with and then go to bed. And try and sleep, despite the noise.

What an amazing place!

Andie looked at what she'd typed. The exclamation mark belied her eagerness. If anybody read this entry, they didn't need to know that her night wasn't turning out as she'd wished.

Hamilton Island

Hamilton Island is the largest inhabited island in the Whitsundays. It's also one of the few that has its own airport. Which is a key reason it gets lots of visitors as they can fly direct. There's plenty of accommodation on offer and a variety of activities to keep you occupied. Tomorrow we're heading out to the reef to go snorkelling. I'm sure Jen will have plenty of photographic evidence of that!

She knew she should add more, but that was as much as she could muster. She'd pad out the entry later with some of the photos Jen took during the day and add captions underneath. That would give a good enough overview of the hours they'd spent so far on the island.

Andie shut down the laptop and turned off the light. Craig had rolled over onto his stomach, which muffled the snoring. As she looked at him, taking up more than his share of the bed, she couldn't help wondering again if what she had was enough.

It took her a long time to fall asleep. Just before she nodded off, she wondered how Jen was going and if she'd taken a walk like she said she would after putting Robert to bed.

The answer to that was yes, but she'd walked for longer than she'd planned to make sure Robert was well and truly asleep. Although, given how much he'd had to drink, he was likely to stay passed out until the morning.

As she walked, Jen wondered how she'd ended up where she was. And where had the man she'd fallen in love with gone? Jen knew she should have gone with Andie and helped with the blog, but she'd needed some fresh air. And to be alone.

Finding a spot on the beach, she sat on the cool, soft sand and tried to decide what to do. It would have been so romantic if Robert had been there with her. They could have walked along the sand, the moonlight above. Held hands. Kissed. Instead, he'd got drunk with Craig and fell asleep.

Initially, she'd been happy that Robert and Craig had decided to spend time together. They used to be close, but in recent years, that had changed. So it had been pleasing seeing them together again. And getting along. But that was before their afternoon of drinking had precluded any plans Jen might have had to spend time with her husband.

'Have you ever been snorkelling before?' Andie asked Jen the next morning as they boarded the boat. 'I can't remember if you've told me.'

'Years ago, on our honeymoon. We haven't snorkelled since.'

'That's right. You went to Fiji, didn't you?'

'Yes, we did.'

Jen remembered their honeymoon vividly. Before they'd left, they had images in their minds of a romantic, tropical paradise. Not unlike the one they were staying in now, Jen thought ruefully. But all they could afford at the time had been a room in a resort with three hundred rooms and a pool that was always swarming with kids. The irony was that they could afford to stay anywhere they wanted now, but they hadn't gone anywhere like that for years.

'I wouldn't mind going to Fiji one day,' Andie said, knowing that as she said it, she'd have a hard time talking Craig into it. To him, the ideal overseas destination was Bali, with its $1 beers. Although maybe she didn't have to go with Craig.

Andie couldn't wait to get in the water and feel it against her skin, and she soon had her wish, jumping off the back of the boat, goggles and snorkel firmly in place. Even though it was autumn, the water wasn't cold. She began to swim slowly, focused on what she was seeing beneath her—stunning coral reefs and a myriad of colourful fish. But after a while, she began to swim away from the group. Not far enough away that the boat crew would start to worry and tell her to come back. Just far enough that she wouldn't have to talk to anyone. She looked over at Craig, but he was focused on what he was doing and didn't see her. He hadn't looked around once to see where she was. Andie sighed and started to swim back. She wasn't going to let her thoughts ruin her time in this breathtaking place.

'I could stay here all day,' Jen said as Andie swam up beside her.

Andie pushed the snorkel aside and laughed. 'You might get tired from treading water after a while.'

'I'd get an inflatable mattress and lie on it. You could join me.'

Andie pictured the two of them bobbing about, each on a floating mattress, under the clear blue sky. It was a mesmerising vision that didn't last long as Robert interrupted her thoughts.

'Can you believe this? It's beautiful down there.'

Jen turned to look at him. 'I thought you weren't a fan of nature.'

'It's just some parts I don't like. Not this though. The reef is spectacular.'

'Have to agree there,' Craig said. 'It will be hard to leave this behind and go inland again. Via Bowen.'

Robert turned to look at him.

'I think it's time to get back on the boat,' Jen said before Robert could say anything.

Back on the boat, they were all tired, having spent the whole time in the water and being the last ones to get out.

'How do you think we can get them to agree on the next part of the trip?' Jen said as they stood at the rear of the boat, looking at the ocean as they headed back to shore.

Andie smiled. 'Toss a coin.'

Our first full day on Hamilton Island was wonderful, with most of it spent out on the reef snorkelling. As well as the stunning beauty under the azure water, there was also beauty above the water in this picturesque spot in the Coral Sea. It's been years since we have been to the Great Barrier Reef, and even today, we only saw a small part of the 2900 individual reefs and 900 islands. There is no way we could have seen the entirety, which stretches over 2,300 kilometres, in one day unless we flew over it. But then, we wouldn't have been able to immerse ourselves in the tropical water.

'You're so good at that,' Jen said, reading over Andie's shoulder. 'I'm sure our friends and families are enjoying the entries.'

Andie still wasn't sure about that. She couldn't think of anyone she knew that didn't spend their days juggling various commitments, leaving very little time for themselves. Reading about their trip around Australia was probably low on the list of priorities. But if nothing else, they'd have a good record of their adventure.

The next day, the ferry back to Airlie Beach didn't leave until 4 pm, so Robert decided it was the perfect time for a game of golf. None of them had played before, but Robert had spoken about playing for years. The golf course was on a different island, so they jumped on the boat and headed over.

'Golf,' Craig muttered as they zipped across the ocean. 'Really?'

'Why not?' Andie said. 'We may as well give it a go. There'll be plenty of things on this trip that we've never done before.'

'I suppose you're right,' Craig said, still looking sceptical.

'And besides, you'll get to drive another golf cart.'

That put a smile on his face. But not for long. By the time the boat arrived at their destination, Craig was beginning to change his mind.

'Why do I have to dress like this? I look stupid.'

'You don't look stupid. Let's go.'

Robert had loaned Craig one of his polo shirts. Andie suspected it was this, and not how he looked, that made him uncomfortable. As much as she tried to understand the dynamic between them, she was still confused about why Craig was ok with Robert one minute but not the next.

Within thirty minutes of teeing off, Andie realised the only thing Craig would enjoy was driving the cart. 'Where the hell has the ball gone this time?' he said.

'I think it landed in the sand bunker,' Robert said, pointing to his left.

'Bloody hell.'

Andie sighed. 'It was just one bad shot. You don't need to carry on.'

'Andie's right,' Jen said. 'I had some terrible shots on the last hole, but I'm doing really well on this one.'

'Well, aren't you lucky,' Craig said.

Andie turned to him. 'Shut up and keep playing.'

'I don't want to. This is a stupid game.'

Jen and Andie watched as Craig strode towards the sand bunker, club gripped tightly in his hand.

'I'm sure he'll enjoy it eventually,' Jen said.

Andie shook her head. 'He's made up his mind and won't change it.'

'Are you having fun?'

Andie nodded. 'What about you?'

'I am, and so is Robert. He's already talking about taking it up when we get home.'

Jen left out the part where she hadn't agreed yet. Thinking about what would happen after the trip was something she wasn't ready to focus on. There were too many conflicting thoughts about the future running through her head. To distract her, she watched Craig try to hit the ball out of the sand bunker. For the third time.

'That's not going to help, is it?'

Andie shook her head and then sighed. 'No, it's not. I guess we should probably go over to where he is.'

Robert was already standing on the green. For someone who wasn't very sporty, golf came naturally to him.

'Isn't this a great game,' Robert called out after Craig finally managed to hit the ball out.

Craig shook his head. 'No.'

'It was just a bad shot. Don't let that put you off.'

'I wish everyone would stop staying that.'

'Well, it's true.'

Craig didn't reply. He just glared as Robert putted his ball in. It took Craig two putts to do the same, even though it had been closer to the hole than Robert's.

'How much longer do we have to do this?' Craig asked as he and Andie climbed back into the cart.

'There are six holes to go,' Andie said.

The look on his face told Andie exactly what he thought about that, but, just for clarification, he said loudly how much he hated the game.

It was at that point Andie's patience ran out. 'Too bad. We haven't finished yet, so you'll just have to stick with it.'

'I don't want to.'

'You don't have a choice.'

'Yes, I do. I could go back to the clubhouse now.'

'Where you'd have a beer, no doubt.'

'Now there's an idea.'

'No, it's not. I want to keep playing.'

'So why do I have to stay?'

'Because I need the cart. And it would be nice to do this together.'

Craig didn't respond but drove on to the next hole, where he started complaining again.

'Whoever invented this game is an idiot.'

Andie watched as he stormed off to where his ball had landed. She watched as he hit it. And she watched as it ended up in the water.

'I'm done. I'm going back.'

He left the clubs on the back of the cart and started walking towards the clubhouse in the distance. He almost got hit by a ball when he walked across a fairway that others were playing on.

As she watched him leave, she found it hard to stop seething about his behaviour. So much so she had to take several deep breaths before continuing to play the game. But thirty minutes later, she was still angry about his behaviour and the fact that he was ruining her game. Then, she saw something from the corner of her eye. Dolphins. A pod of them in the ocean to her right. She stopped and watched them as they gracefully arced out of the water and then back under. Watching them made her realise there were better things to think about than Craig's tantrum. And they also reminded her that the ocean had again, come to her rescue.

When they finished playing, they went to find Craig. But he wasn't in the clubhouse. He'd gone back to the main island and planted himself at the bar.

'You should've kept going,' Robert said. 'You would have got the hang of it.'

Only Andie saw the look that quickly passed across his face.

'I'd rather be here.'

'But you gave up. Didn't you want to succeed at it?'

This time Jen saw the look as well. 'So, is there anything else we should do before the boat returns to the mainland?'

'I wouldn't mind going for one more swim,' Andie said. 'The water is so beautiful.'

Jen nodded. 'Great idea. I'll be in that. Are you two coming?'

Craig shook his head and took another sip of his beer. Robert shook his head too, before heading to the bar. Andie could only assume he hadn't noticed the look on Craig's face; otherwise, why was he staying?

As Andie floated in the ocean, looking up at the sky, she wished she could stay there by herself and never have to deal with Craig again. To her left, Jen was also floating. She was quiet though, and hadn't made any attempt at conversation.

They stayed in the water until the last possible moment before getting out so they could change for the boat ride back.

No one had booked the rooms they were in, so they'd organised a late checkout. Craig was waiting when Andie got back.

'Enjoy your swim?'

She could tell by the tone of his voice that he was looking for a fight. She wasn't going to give him one.

'Yes,' she said, walking into the bathroom and shutting the door.

Andie stayed in the bathroom as long as she could but eventually, she had to come out, or they'd miss the boat.

'What's his problem?' Craig said as soon as she'd opened the door. 'Rob can be such a dick sometimes.'

'Let it go,' Andie said, not looking in his direction.

'I'm not talking to him on the boat.'

Andie sighed. Was he five years old again? She said nothing though, and they headed down to the marina. True to his word, he went off on his own and stayed away from Robert on the trip back. So much for them getting along, she thought to herself.

Later that afternoon, as they sat outside their caravans, Craig pulled a coin out of his wallet.

Robert looked at him. 'What are you doing?'

'Tossing a coin to decide which direction we're going. Heads we go inland via Bowen, tails we don't.'

Robert took a sip of his wine. 'I still think this is a silly idea. The route we originally planned will take us to the inland towns without adding more time by going north then west.'

'We're tossing the coin,' Jen said, hands on her hips. 'We want to go north then inland, but you won't agree.'

'I just don't think there is much worth seeing in Bowen, so it makes no sense to add it to our drive.'

'I'm sure there'll be plenty to see,' Jen said, this time folding her arms. 'We shouldn't even be doing this. You're outvoted. If you weren't so stubborn, we'd just be going.'

'I'm not being stubborn. I think it's a waste of time.'

Jen glared at him before turning to Craig. 'Toss the coin.'

Three heads turned to watch him as he tossed it in the air and let it fall to the ground.

Craig grinned. 'Heads it is. We're going to Bowen.'

Robert didn't say anything but turned and walked over to top up his wine.

'Let's start planning the stops,' Craig said.

Five minutes later, Andie, Craig and Jen were looking at the map. Craig was still grinning, and Andie wished he would stop. Andie turned her attention to her laptop instead.

We didn't realise until we checked the map how close Bowen is – only 76 kilometres north of where we are. A slight detour to our original itinerary to see another town in our home state. So, our new route is – from Bowen, we'll go inland to Collinsville. From there, we'll go south to Clermont, drive through Alpha, Barcaldine, Longreach, Winton, Cloncurry, Julia Creek, Hughenden, Charters Towers and on to Townsville.

Looking at the map, there are unsealed roads, and we discussed whether they would be suitable for our caravans. But it seems they're all compacted dirt, so we should be fine. It's exciting that we've made a slight change to the itinerary. That's part of the adventure of this trip. Adding new places and seeing what we find.

As Andie looked at what she'd written, it wasn't exactly the truth. Three of them were excited. She didn't know when Robert would get out of the mood he was in.

Chapter Six

'What a lovely town,' Andie said as they drove along the streets of Bowen the following morning.

Craig nodded. 'I don't know what Rob's problem is. Why wouldn't he want to stop here?'

Andie shrugged. And she was just about to remind him that it was Robert, not Rob, when her phone beeped.'

There's something called the Big Mango. We have to go there.

Andie grinned as she replied to Jen.

I assume you'll be wanting a photo.

Absolutely! I'm going to get a photo of all the 'big' things we come across. And we should do a feature on our blog!

Andie reread the last sentence before saying no in her head. She knew Jen was excited about their blog, but Andie didn't want to spend more time than needed documenting the towns they would visit. Feature stories were a step too far.

'There's the caravan park,' Craig said, pointing to the left, interrupting her thoughts.

'This has been the easiest drive so far.'

Craig nodded. 'I wish they could all be like this.'

'You're not over the driving already, are you? We've only just started.'

Craig shook his head. 'No, but there'll be times when we'll have to drive all day just to get to the next destination.'

Andie turned to look out the window. Long distances meant long periods spent in the car together. Just the two of them. With no one else to talk to. And plenty of time for Andie's thoughts about their marriage to take over.

'I've done some research,' Jen said an hour later once they'd set up. 'Apart from the Big Mango, we should also visit Horseshoe Bay and Queens Beach.'

Andie nodded. 'Sounds like a plan.'

'I might stay here,' Robert said. 'I'm not feeling the best. I think I'll just rest.'

Jen turned to him. 'What's wrong? You didn't mention feeling unwell in the car.'

'It's just come on now. I must have eaten something that didn't agree with me.'

'We all had the same thing for breakfast,' Jen said. 'And we're all fine.'

Robert shrugged. 'Maybe it wasn't food. I don't know. I just don't want to go wandering around.'

'But you'll miss out on seeing the town.'

'That's all right. You go with Craig and Andie. You can tell me about it later.'

Jen turned back to look at their caravan site. The chair Robert had been sitting in only a few moments before was now empty. She knew him well enough to know he wasn't sick. She shook her head, making sure Andie and Craig didn't see her and continued walking.

They hadn't even left their own state yet, and already he was acting like a spoilt child. Just because he didn't get his own way. Did he have any idea how unhappy she was feeling? And what she was hoping this trip would do?

'Can you take a photo of me in front of the mango?' Jen said ten minutes later, giving Andie her phone. 'If I try and take a selfie, I'll end up cutting off the top.'

Andie laughed. 'The top of the mango or the top of you?'

Jen poked her tongue out. 'The mango, of course.'

Andie looked at Jen as she took the photo. Jen looked happy, grinning as she stood in front of the mango, but something wasn't right. Andie just couldn't put her finger on what gave her that impression. Andie hoped Jen would be ok.

That she and Robert would be ok. Which was ironic considering she was in turmoil about her own marriage.

When they returned in the late afternoon, Robert was sitting in a chair looking out at the ocean, a glass of wine in his hand. From the look in his eyes, they could tell it wasn't his first for the day. Craig said he'd join Robert as soon as he'd had a shower and headed towards the amenities block.

'I thought you weren't feeling well,' Jen said. 'Wine won't help, you know.'

'It's helping. A lot. I feel much better now.'

'I don't think you were ever sick.'

Robert waited a moment before speaking. 'Not physically sick. Just not in the right frame of mind to be here again.'

'Again?' Jen said. 'When were you in Bowen?'

'A long time ago. When I was a child.'

'So why didn't you want to come here now? Did something happen the last time you were here?'

'I don't want to talk about it.'

'Why not?' Jen said.

'I don't feel up to it. Can we leave it for now?'

Jen could tell he was getting upset, so she didn't say anything else. Instead, she watched him get up, walk out of the caravan park and onto the beach.

Andie watched him go as well, intrigued by what he'd said and curious about what he hadn't. It wasn't the right time to mention it though. So rather than say anything about Robert, she turned to Jen and asked what she wanted to do for dinner.

'I think we should stay here. Taking him out anywhere isn't a good idea.'

Andie nodded in agreement. A night in would be good for their budget too.

While Robert was away, Andie did a quick update on the day's activities.

Bowen

Standing in front of the Big Mango, we could see how it got its name. It's 10 metres high! We didn't find out whose idea it was to build it but considering that the Bowen Mango is one of the most well-known items to come from the area, it's not surprising that it was built. And we all love mangoes, especially the ones that come from Bowen! Unfortunately, we're here out of season. We did get to try a mango sorbet though.

As Andie typed, she thought it best not to mention that Robert hadn't been part of their excursion.

We also visited Horseshoe Bay, known as Bowen's most iconic beach. At either end, two granite outcrops frame the beach. And luckily, we had our swimmers with us as not far from the shore, we got to see an incredible range of fish and coral. If we'd had time, we could have hired some snorkelling equipment and explored further. But we needed to head to Queens Bay for a walk along its five kilometres of sandy beach.

Andie looked up from the screen. She decided to leave out the part where Craig whinged about walking and sat himself down while she and Jen continued. She was about to go back to the blog entry when Robert came back, and she decided it would be better to keep Jen company. She'd already started preparing the salad to go with the meat they would soon barbeque.

Dinner was eaten mostly in silence. Robert was more interested in the glass in his hand, and Craig was going over the next day's journey. He didn't notice Robert's disposition. Andie and Jen spoke, but only occasionally. The mood around the table wasn't conducive to animated conversation.

After dinner, Craig decided to go to bed. 'We've got a big day tomorrow, so I'm going to turn in. See you all in the morning.'

No one else was tired, so they continued sitting around the table. Andie started to feel uncomfortable and was preparing to get up and leave when Jen broke the silence.

'Do you feel up to talking?' Jen said, taking hold of Robert's hand.

Robert stayed silent.

'I can go if you want,' Andie said.

Robert shook his head. 'It doesn't matter if you hear.'

Andie wasn't sure if it was the alcohol or whether Robert was ready to talk, but after a few minutes, he began speaking.

'Back in primary school, I played soccer for a while. The team I was in won the southeast Queensland schools' competition. Because of that, we were sponsored to come up here to play the team that won the north Queensland schools' competition. I hadn't been to north Queensland before, so I was excited. And my best friend was on the trip, which made it even better.'

For the next ten minutes, Robert continued. After his team won the game, they celebrated with pizzas and soft drinks. Their coach had the ball they'd used in the game and was taking photos of each of the boys holding it. When it was thrown to Robert's best friend, he missed it and chased after it onto the street. Robert could still remember the thud and then the screaming that followed. To this day, Robert could still clearly see his best friend lying in the street, his eyes open in surprise but not seeing anything.

'As soon as we drove into town, every detail came flooding back. I doubt the pizza place is still here, but I don't want to go anywhere near the road where it happened.'

Jen put her arms around him. 'I'm so sorry you had to experience that.'

'No matter how many years go by, I've never forgotten.'

As he said it, Robert looked like he was about to cry. Andie got up quietly and left the two of them alone.

Chapter Seven

The following morning, Andie asked Craig why he'd gone to bed so early.

'Robert was annoying me. Just because he didn't get his own way and we came here. I'm sure he sat around and sulked while we were gone.'

It wasn't Andie's story to tell, but she shared what Robert had said anyway. She needed to set Craig straight.

'That's a long time ago now,' he said in response. 'You'd think he'd be over it.'

Andie sighed. 'Well, he's not, and it's none of our business.'

Craig was about to say something else but the look on Andie's face stopped him. She then looked out the caravan window and saw that Jen and Robert were almost ready to go.

'Come on,' Andie said. 'We need to hurry up.'

Within half an hour, they were on the road for the 85-kilometre trip to Collinsville. They planned to look around and then continue another 356 kilometres to Clermont.

Jen and Robert were in front, with Andie and Craig not far behind. Jen had been looking out the window, but the closer they got to Collinsville, the less there was to see. Just dirt and a few trees. So instead, she researched what they could do when they arrived. As far as attractions go, there was a coal mining museum, which is understandable given that Collinsville was a coal mining town. And the hinterland was supposed to be picturesque, so that was two things they could do, as well as look around the town itself. She put down her phone and stared out the window again, not expecting to see anything different. So, she was surprised when she did.

'Look,' she exclaimed, pointing to her left.

'I can't,' Robert said. 'I'm driving.'

'You only need to glance sideways for a second.'

'What's that doing out here by itself?' Robert asked, spotting the solitary camel standing on a hill, its eyes fixed on the road. 'It reminds me of that lone dingo on Fraser Island that was staring at us.'

The one I didn't get to see, Jen was about to say before thinking the better of it. The one where you dismissed my feelings. Like you've done more times than I want to remember. She kept those last thoughts to herself as well. She didn't have the energy to deal with how he would react.

'No idea,' she said instead. 'But at least it's something different to look at.'

Jen continued to scan the landscape to see if any other camels appeared, but none did. She told Andie and Craig about it when they pulled up.

Andie nodded. 'We saw it too.'

'It was the only thing to look at on the way,' Robert grumbled.

'That's the point,' Craig said. 'It's so different to what we're used to. Being out here is going to be great.'

Robert scowled. 'I'd rather be in the city.'

'We may as well look around now that we're here,' Andie said quickly before either Craig or Robert continued down the path they were starting on.

Jen nodded in agreement. 'How about we do the museum, walk around town, have an early lunch and then look at the hinterland as we leave?'

'Good idea,' Andie said. 'Let's go.'

Their morning itinerary didn't take long to complete, which was good because Craig said he was hungry at least three times.

'There's a pub just up ahead,' Craig said. 'I'm sure they do lunch.'

Not long after they'd ordered, Robert went up to the bar and bought a round of drinks—a beer and three wines. Then, behind them, they heard a male voice.

'What's he drinking that for?'

Jen leaned over and touched Robert's hand. 'Ignore them.'

Craig turned to look in the direction of the voice. He saw two men with beers in front of them, dressed in the same clothes they'd worn during their shift at the mine nearby.

'What sort of man drinks that shit?' the other said.

This time Robert turned around to look at them.

'What are you staring at?' the first one said before his mate chimed in.

'Go back to your lady's drink.'

'Don't say anything, Robert,' Jen said.

The first one laughed. 'Yeah, do what your wife says.'

Robert got up from the table.

Jen reached out for him. 'Don't.'

'Keep your opinions to yourself,' Robert said to them. 'No one is interested.'

'We can say what we like,' the mate said. 'This is our local. We're here all the time.'

'Not surprised,' Robert said. 'You're probably not allowed anywhere else in town.'

Both men put their beers down and stood up, turning to face Robert. Craig pushed back his chair and got to his feet. He was bigger than both of them.

'Why don't you sit back down,' Craig said.

The four men stared at each other, and no one spoke. Eventually, the two locals sat back down.

'Here comes our lunch,' Craig said, breaking the tension.

As they ate, Andie kept glancing over at Craig. Even though he'd never gone looking for a fight, over the years, he'd stepped in if he needed to. And he usually won. She was glad it hadn't come to that. It was nice to see Craig standing up for Robert though.

Jen also thought it was nice that Craig had been there for Robert. And even though it wasn't the best circumstance, it had also been nice to see a glimpse of the old Robert.

They ate mostly in silence, and after they'd finished their lunch, they left straight away.

'Thanks for that,' Robert said when they were outside. 'I could have handled it myself though.'

Craig nodded. 'I know, but there were two of them, so it made sense to even things up.'

Robert nodded, and then they headed back towards their cars to drive out to the hinterland and then on to Clermont.

'This looks more promising,' Robert said after they arrived and set up just under four hours later. 'Haven't seen anyone yet who looks like those two back at lunch.'

'There are people like that everywhere,' Jen said. 'Why are those two bothering you so much?'

'They're not bothering me,' Robert said. 'I just couldn't let them get away with what they said about me.'

'Well, I'm glad nothing happened. You haven't been in a fight since you were a drunk twenty-five-year-old.'

'I can still hold my own.'

Jen looked at his middle-aged body, which hadn't done regular exercise for a long time. 'I doubt that.'

From where Andie was standing, she watched Robert open the caravan door and stomp inside. She wanted to look around but decided to wait a few minutes and let Robert calm down before suggesting it. Instead, she opened the door of their caravan and headed in.

'So, Robert thinks he would have been all right on his own?' Craig said before she'd even had the chance to shut the door.

Andie sighed. 'Don't say anything.'

Craig paused for a moment. 'I guess you're right. I shouldn't say anything.'

Now it was Andie's turn to pause, wondering why Craig had let it drop so easily. She was going to ask but decided not to. Instead, she suggested they go to the tourist information centre.

Before leaving, Andie looked through the window and saw the door to Jen and Robert's caravan was still shut, and Jen was nowhere in sight. So, she and Craig went to the building with the large blue 'I' out the front on their own.

'Good morning,' said a cheerful voice from behind the counter. 'How are you today?'

'Good, thank you.' Andie replied, looking at the badge on the woman in front of her, which displayed the name Patricia.

'Have you travelled far today?'

'Just from Collinsville.'

'Only a short drive then. So, I'm guessing you'd like to know what there is to see in our lovely town?'

Andie nodded.

'Let me get a map and mark a few things for you. Are you on holiday?'

Andie nodded again and told her about their trip.

'What a great thing to do at your age. We get a lot of grey nomads and young backpackers, but not many your age.'

'We're too old to be sleeping in bunk beds in a room with other people,' Craig said as he came to stand behind Andie.

Andie nodded. 'Besides, listening to your snoring is enough. I don't want to put up with other people snoring.'

Craig turned to look at her. 'Gee, thanks.'

Patricia smiled. 'I would have liked to do what you're doing, but I'm too old now. And to set in my ways.'

'I'm sure you could still go if you wanted to,' Andie said.

Patricia shook her head. 'At my age, I'm content to stay here. It's my home.'

'How long have you lived here?' Andie said.

'All my life. I grew up on a property just outside town and moved into town when I got married.'

'How long have you been married?'

'I was married for forty-two years. My husband died last year.'

'I'm sorry to hear that.'

'All those years working in the mines. I don't think it did much for his long-term health.'

'So, what is there to see in town?' Craig said.

Andie gave him a gentle kick to the ankle that Patricia couldn't see.

'What?' he said.

Patricia spread the map out in front of them and pointed out the places of interest while Andie noted what they should do. Craig stared out the window.

'Enjoy your stay,' Patricia said as they turned to leave.

Andie smiled at her. 'We will.'

Outside Craig turned to Andie. 'Why did you kick me?'

'To get you to stop talking.'

'Why?'

'She was talking about her husband who died. Couldn't you see how sad she looked?'

Craig shook his head. 'I didn't notice.'

Andie sighed. 'Of course, you didn't. Let's find Jen and Robert.'

When they got back, the caravan door was still closed, and Andie assumed the others were inside.

'How long do we leave them?' Craig said. 'I've spent enough time sitting today during that drive. I want to go and look at things.'

'Maybe another ten minutes. If the door is still shut, then we'll knock.'

But they didn't need to. Five minutes later, the door opened. And Andie could tell that Jen had redressed herself in a hurry.

'Wonder what you were doing?' Andie said with a smile.

Jen blushed. 'Nothing we need to talk about in public.'

'I would have thought the drama at the pub would have had the opposite effect.'

'So did I. And it did at first. But then his mood changed.'

'I wonder why?'

Jen shook her head. 'No idea. But I wasn't questioning it. It's been a while.'

Andie almost said it was the same for her, but something stopped her. She didn't have the energy to talk about it. She wasn't even sure she wanted to.

The light was beginning to fade, the sun slowly setting, not leaving much time in the daylight hours to explore. At least they managed to walk along the main street before the light faded completely. The rest of the sightseeing could wait until the following day.

By mid-afternoon the next day, they'd seen everything Patricia had recommended, and they found a spot by a lagoon to have afternoon tea. Andie and Jen were happy with coffee. Craig wanted a beer. So did Robert. Jen and Andie watched him as he opened it.

'What?' Robert said. 'I've started acquiring a taste for it since we started the trip.'

Andie turned to look at Craig. 'Did you bring anything else?'

Craig shook his head. 'I thought you just wanted coffee.'

'That's only because Jen thought to make some and put it in a thermos. I wouldn't have minded a cold drink.'

'I had a wine in our esky, but Jen took it out,' Robert said.

'We don't need to drink alcohol every time we stop somewhere,' Jen said.

Robert turned to look at her. 'I'm on holiday.'

'Don't use that excuse,' Jen said.

Andie could see the look on Jen's face and decided to change the subject.

'This is a lovely spot,' she said, looking at the water in front of them, the trees surrounding them and the wispy, white clouds in the sky. Apart from the four of them, there were no other people in the vicinity. It was the first time since they'd left the coast that Andie had felt the peace that had materialised in other locations. But like every other time, it was fleeting.

Andie turned back to look at the others. 'So where are we off to tomorrow?'

'Barcaldine,' Craig said. 'It's just over four hours from here, and I think the road's a bit rough in places.'

The look on Robert's face told them how he felt about tomorrow's drive. Just like the look on Jen's face told them how she felt when Craig mentioned they'd be stopping at the Gemfields on the way. It wasn't just her grin. Her eyes lit up at the thought of gems. She'd always loved jewellery and had an extensive collection. Andie didn't say anything. There was no money in the budget for things like that. She wondered if they should have delayed the trip until they'd saved more, but Craig had wanted to go now. The budget they'd need had never crossed his mind. It was Andie who took care of their finances and juggled their funds between accounts to make sure everything was paid on time. It wouldn't cross his mind either that occasionally, she might like a new piece of jewellery.

It hadn't always been like that. When Craig first started his business, it had been booming. But a downturn in the real estate market had changed that. Andie remembered the holidays they used to take, the weekends away, the dinners. Craig and his crew worked seven days a week to keep up with demand. But then interest rates went up, and people started losing their homes. And stopped building new ones. Even though work eventually picked up, it never got to those heights again. They always had enough to get by, but they couldn't splurge like they once had, and a part of Andie missed it. Especially when there were constant reminders around her of what extra money allowed you to do.

That night, they had dinner at the caravan park. To everyone's surprise, it was Robert who suggested it. Which Andie assumed was because he didn't want to go to the pub in case some locals didn't agree with his usual drink of choice again. But not going to the pub didn't stop him from drinking. As soon as they returned from their day out, he'd opened a wine. By the time they'd finished dinner, he was on to his second bottle. Andie could see Jen watching him, but she didn't say anything. Craig did though.

'You're knocking those back tonight.'

'Just relaxing.'

'Too much more, and you won't be relaxing, you'll be sleeping.'

'No, I won't. I'll be fine.'

'We've got an early start in the morning.'

'Then I better go inside.'

They watched him get up and go into the caravan with the wine bottle in his hand.

Andie turned to Craig. 'Why did you do that?'

'What?'

Andie sighed. Sometimes he had no clue.

Instead, she turned to Jen. 'Is he all right?'

Jen shrugged. 'I don't know what's got into him.'

Andie watched as Jen got up and walked into their caravan.

'I might go inside too,' Andie said.

'I'll be in a bit later,' Craig said, not looking up from the sports update he was checking on his phone.

Off to bed on my own again, Andie thought as she shut the door.

The next morning, they set off early, and after driving for an hour, they reached the town of Rubyvale in the Gemfields. Robert swore he didn't have a hangover, but by the look of him, it was clear that he did.

'This isn't what I thought it would be,' Jen said, looking around the small town, with its scattered single-storey buildings and a lone bitumen road dividing the town, all surrounded by a dry landscape.

'What were you expecting?' Andie said.

'I was picturing something like one of those old-fashioned gold rush towns. You know, the ones where people dress in costumes and ride in stagecoaches pulled by horses.'

Andie laughed. 'What made you think that?'

Jen shrugged. 'The name, I guess. And where are the gems?'

Craig turned to look at her. 'In the ground. You have to go fossicking for them.'

Andie could tell Jen was deciding whether or not she wanted to spend a few hours digging in the dirt, at the end of which she probably wouldn't have found a gem. So instead, she proposed they go for a drive and see if anyone was already in the fields fossicking.

Robert wasn't interested. 'There must be something else to do.'

'I'm sure there is,' Craig said. 'But I'd like to see if anyone is fossicking.'

Robert looked like he was about to disagree but then stopped himself just before he was about to speak.

'How about we look around first and then go to the fields on the way out of town?' Jen suggested.

It didn't take them long to wander around, and soon they were heading out to the fields. But to everyone's disappointment, except Robert's, they didn't see anyone fossicking. They did find a spot with a good view of the surrounding area, and Jen wanted a photo, so they stopped. And then they heard a voice.

'What are you taking photos of? This is my area.'

Behind them stood a man holding a shotgun. He looked like he hadn't showered in days. Or visited a dentist in a while, as a few of his teeth were missing.

'We're just taking a photo of the view,' Craig said.

'How do I know you're not lying? You could be here to try and steal my claims.'

'Why would we do that?' Craig said.

'Lots of people try.'

They all looked at each other and then looked at the shotgun. No one said anything for several seconds until Craig spoke up again.

'If we were after your claim, wouldn't we have brought some fossicking tools with us? We've got nothing. As I said, we just wanted a photo.'

The man looked at them but didn't put the shotgun down. After a minute or two, he spoke.

'I don't know if I believe you. You better get out of here before I change my mind.'

No one argued that point, and soon they were back on the highway and heading towards Barcaldine. It was a three-hour drive, but no one was bothered about that.

Andie looked out the window at the nothingness as they drove. In previous days the nothingness hadn't worried her, but now, she wished other people were around. Craig had handled the situation well, but they'd also been lucky. What if he hadn't listened to Craig's reasoning? Her thoughts were interrupted by a text from Jen.

What the hell was that about?

I don't know, but I don't like what happened.

Me either. What if he'd used his gun?

I've been thinking the same thing.

I'm glad we're out of there.

Me too.

How long to Barcaldine?

Another hour.

Hope it goes quickly.

So do I!

They hadn't been in Barcaldine more than ten minutes before Robert started commenting that they should have listened to him and not gone out to the Gemfields, which didn't go down well with Craig.

'No one could have predicted that was going to happen. And besides, he didn't hurt any of us, and we're all safe.'

'But it might not have turned out that way.'

'Well, it did, so there's no point thinking about it.'

'Why don't we talk about what we're going to do while we're here,' Andie said, interrupting them and feeling exasperated at having to do so. Although, she had to admit that Craig didn't look as annoyed with Robert as he usually was in situations like this.

'According to the Barcaldine tourist information site, there's a lot to see,' Jen chimed in.

As Jen read through the list of things to do, Andie noticed that she also didn't look as annoyed with Robert as she had been lately when he behaved like he just had.

Once they'd decided on the following day's itinerary, they had an early dinner and went to bed. No one felt festive that night.

Our adventures today

Andie thought about the day they'd just had and what points to add to the blog before she resumed typing. She'd already decided to leave out the past few days. The miners at lunch and the man with the gun were things she didn't want to draw attention to. Or be reminded of if she ever reread the blog once the trip was over.

Barcaldine

The Tree of Knowledge was the first place we visited on our Barcaldine sightseeing tour. Well, to be correct, we saw the memorial. The actual tree was poisoned in 2006. There was a lot of discussion between us as to why someone would poison a tree. We checked several news stories but couldn't find a reference to the culprit, so we concluded that maybe it was someone who didn't like the Australian Labor Party, as that's where it was formed back in 1891– under the tree. A quick bit of research (otherwise known as reading the plaque on the memorial) told us there was a shearer's strike that year, and the strike leaders gathered under the tree. And from there, the political party was formed.

Next up, we decided to venture along the Between the Bougainvilleas Heritage Trail, which showcases some of the diverse and colourful history of the area. Even though the sites on the trail are identified by maroon-coloured signs featuring a windmill on each, we still grabbed a booklet outlining the sites from the information centre to make sure we saw everything.

Andie stopped typing and went over the later part of the afternoon in her head.

Booklet purchased, they'd set off, walking and then in their cars. Jen had suggested they go in one car. Craig and Robert both agreed straightaway, something Andie couldn't help but notice. Something had changed in the way they reacted to each other. She couldn't put her finger on it, but she wasn't going to question it.

Jen also noticed, but she didn't say anything either. By the time they'd seen the first few sites on the trail, the only thing her attention was focused on was the photos they found. Many of the sites had a historical photograph and a present-day one side by side

'Then and now,' she'd said.

Andie had noticed a woman in one of the photos, taken over a hundred years ago. She'd peered closely at her face but couldn't tell if she was happy. If anyone looked closely at a photo of Andie, would they be able to know if she was happy. Or not.

When they'd got to the last spot on their Barcaldine itinerary, Robert had started whinging. 'I'm not walking around all two hectares.'

'Don't then,' Jen had said. 'I'm going to see everything there is to see.'

Jen had headed off, and Andie and Craig followed. Robert had waited for a moment before coming along, but he'd stayed a few steps behind the rest of them. They walked around the complex for the next two hours and looked at the exhibitions and stories about Australia's working history. On their way out, they noticed a retail outlet.

Unsurprisingly, we found a retail outlet at the Australian Workers Heritage Centre. Most tourist places have them. They need the extra money that the sales bring to help cover the running costs. So Jen and I bought a small souvenir each.

Andie left out the part where Craig and Robert said it was a waste of money. That the souvenirs would go to the back of a drawer as soon as they got home. And while Andie knew they were right, it wasn't about that. There'd only been three other people there, and they'd both wanted to give something extra. Even though Jen hadn't said anything, Andie could tell by the way she only pointed out the cheaper souvenirs that she had Andie and Craig's budget in mind.

After we visited the workers' centre, we decided to continue to our next stop, Longreach, as it was just over an hour's drive away.

Andie stopped typing again. Robert had initially been happy to move on as he'd said more than once that day that the rural countryside didn't appeal to him. Then he realised they were heading for more of the same. Jen tried to change his opinion by saying she'd heard that Longreach was a lovely town, and she was looking forward to it. For a moment, it seemed like that hadn't worked, but then Robert looked at Jen and stopped his grumbling.

The change had surprised Andie. As had the fact that Craig had kept quiet when he could have easily told Robert it didn't matter what he thought as they were heading to Longreach regardless.

Andie put the laptop down as the others were ready to go. She'd written enough for today anyway.

After setting up the caravans in Longreach, they decided to have dinner at the nearest pub, where Robert didn't bother asking for a wine list. He ordered a beer instead. And the biggest steak on the menu.

'Hope you're hungry,' Jen said to Robert when their meals arrived.

Andie looked at the plate that had been put in front of him. The steak was hanging over the sides, and what wasn't covered by the steak was piled high with chips and salad. And a bowl of mushroom sauce had been placed on the table next to the plate.

'I don't think I've ever seen you order such a big meal,' Jen said.

'I'm hungry.'

Craig looked at the plate. 'Looks like something I usually order. I'll help you finish it if you can't eat it all.'

Robert shook his head. 'I'll manage.'

The others finished their meals long before Robert. Even though they could all see he was struggling, he kept eating until all the steak was gone. And then Andie remembered that back in

Collinsville, the two miners had been eating steak. Huge servings.

The next morning, Jen looked tired.

'Robert was up all-night groaning from stomach pains because of all the food he ate,' she said to Andie.

After breakfast, which Robert didn't eat, they started on their Longreach itinerary. Robert may not have wanted any food, but he was back to organising them. He rushed them off to the Stockmen's Hall of Fame, where they saw displays and audio-visual presentations of outback life, learnt about stockmen and explorers and the local Aboriginal people. From there, they went to the QANTAS Museum, where they learned about the beginnings of the Queensland and Northern Territory Air Service, saw a replica of QANTAS' first-ever aircraft, walked along the wings of a Boeing 747 and went inside the cockpit. They'd only just walked out the museum door when Robert bustled them on to Cobb & Co for a stagecoach ride through the scrub.

'What's with the one-hundred-and-eighty-degree change of mind?' Andie said, still trying to take notes for the blog so she could update it with where they'd been that morning. 'He seems to be very interested.'

Jen shook her head. 'Don't let that fool you. He wants to do everything out here as quickly as possible so we can go back to the coast.'

'It's a paddle wheeler,' Craig said when they got to their last stop of the day, a sunset river cruise. 'I didn't think we'd be going on one of these until we got to the Murray River.'

The late afternoon light over the river was beautiful, as were the last of the sun's rays dancing on the water. They all enjoyed the cruise, even Robert. Jen took so many photos that Andie wasn't sure how much she saw without looking through her phone. At one point, Andie noticed that Robert reached over and put his arm around her, and she put her phone down and leaned into him. Craig was too busy looking at the surrounding landscape to notice. And he didn't put his arm around Andie at any time during the cruise. He didn't try to hold her hand either. When she reached for him, he didn't even notice.

Later that day, as the guys were cooking dinner on the BBQ, Andie added the last points about the river cruise to the blog. She'd already added the rest of the day but had paused to marvel at how well Craig and Robert were getting along that night.

Much to Robert's annoyance, which sometimes he managed to hide, they continued their drive through the outback over the next few days.

149

Winton, Cloncurry, Charters Towers

Our outback adventures have carried on. Most of us are enjoying it. We stopped in Winton, the dinosaur capital of Australia and the home of Waltzing Matilda. Another highlight, which doesn't appear on many tourist websites, is the 'Great Wall of Winton', a 70-metre concrete wall embedded with discarded items around a property owned by one of the locals.

Then on to Cloncurry, where the Royal Flying Doctors was founded and also, as we found out while we were in town, the destination of the first QANTAS flight, something we should have noted at the museum in Longreach but didn't. We continued on to Julia Creek, staying the night before driving further east. We hadn't planned on staying, but it was another five and half hour drive to our last stop before arriving back on the coast, Charters Towers. We were tired after all the driving, so we didn't see much in Julia Creek, but what we did find in this town with a population of 400 was free camping by the creek from where the town gets its name. It wasn't the same as staying by the ocean as we had in other places, but it continued our tradition of staying somewhere with a water view.

Charters Towers was founded in 1871 after the discovery of gold, and the buildings that still stand from around that time are worth visiting. As is the sunset from Towers Hill. Luckily, the rain that had greeted us as we drove into town cleared, and the sun came out in time for us to see it retire for the day. Going to a drive-in was something else we got to do in Charters Towers that none of us had done in a long time. The drive-in is one of the oldest in Queensland and only one of four still in operation (so says Google).

As they packed up the morning after their movie under the stars, Andie noticed that Robert could barely keep the smile off his face, and she was pleased that he was starting to enjoy himself in the outback. Until she realised he was thinking of their next stop, Townsville, which was back on the coast. And back on his original itinerary.

Chapter Eight

As they came into Townsville, Andie looked up and saw Castle Hill. She texted Jen.

The view from up there will be great.

Yes, it will. I'll have to take lots of photos.

We might have to drive up though. I don't think I can talk Craig into walking up!

Ha! I don't think I could talk Robert into it either. But I'd like to walk up if we can. I could use some more exercise after sitting so much on the long drives.

'This is a nice spot,' Andie said, looking out at the view from their caravan park in Rowes Bay, chosen because it was next to the ocean. 'It will be nice to stay here for a few days.'

Robert nodded in agreement. 'Should be plenty to do.'

'What shall we do first?' Jen asked.

'I wouldn't mind some lunch,' Craig said.

'Let's go down to the Strand,' Robert said. 'There will be somewhere there that does a good lunch.'

'And we could go for a walk afterwards,' Jen said.

'Good choice Robert,' Jen said when they were seated. 'There are some great options on the menu.'

Robert looked pleased with himself at Jen's comment.

'As long as they do a steak,' Craig said.

Andie turned to look at him. 'You could try something else for once.'

'But I like steak.'

'The salmon sounds good,' Jen said.

Robert nodded. 'I was looking at that too.'

Andie smiled to herself. Robert was back to his usual dining habits.

'And a nice glass of pinot grigio to go with it.'

Andie smiled again. No more beer, then.

'So, what's the plan for tomorrow?' Andie asked.

'If it's sunny, we should go to Magnetic Island,' Jen said. 'I went there years ago, and it was lovely.'

'Sounds good to me,' Andie quickly said before Craig could comment about going to another island. 'What about tonight?'

'Let's go to the casino,' Robert said.

'I don't like gambling,' Jen said. 'It's boring, and you're just throwing away money.'

Andie nodded. 'I'm not a big fan either.'

And we can't afford it, she thought to herself.

'There's one here, and it's something we haven't done on this trip,' Craig said. 'I wouldn't mind going to have a look.'

'Great,' Robert said. 'That's sorted.'

Andie looked at him. Clearly, she and Jen didn't get a say. But Craig and Robert agreed on something, so she left it.

As soon as they arrived that night, Craig and Robert went to try their luck at the tables while Andie and Jen went to the bar. Andie had given Craig fifty dollars and told him that was his limit. For some reason, they seemed to be over their budget, even though she'd been careful about what they'd spent. But when she'd looked in her purse that afternoon, there was less money than there should have been, and she couldn't remember where it had been spent. Andie sighed as she thought about it. Sometimes she wished she didn't have to worry about money. At least they were having dinner at the buffet. Much to Robert's irritation. But it was cheaper than the a la carte restaurant. Even at the bar, she was looking for the cheapest drink on the menu. She didn't realise that Jen had bought her a cocktail.

'May as well have one of these, seeing as we've dressed up for the first time on this trip,' Jen said, handing Andie the cocktail.

'You didn't have to do that.'

Jen smiled. 'I wanted to. Besides, it was Robert's idea to come here in the first place, and you and I didn't get much of a say.'

Andie smiled too. 'I guess we can't have everything our way.'

Jen laughed. 'Even though we'd like everything our way. Craig seems to be in a good mood though.'

Andie sighed. 'He likes going to a casino. He doesn't get to go very often because it's not in the budget.'

Jen reached over and squeezed Andie's hand. She always had a way of acknowledging and acting on the differences in their financial situations without doing anything that would make Andie feel uncomfortable. Like buying her just one drink. Which was so delicious she finished it in record time.

'Ready for dinner?' Jen said.

Andie nodded. 'Let's go find the guys.'

Their search led them to the Blackjack table. Robert had chips in front of him. Craig didn't.

'Time to eat,' Jen said. 'We're hungry.'

Robert nodded. Craig wanted to play one more hand.

'Let's just go to dinner,' Robert said. 'You've already lost one hundred and fifty dollars. You don't want to lose anymore.'

Andie turned to look at Craig. 'You lost one hundred and fifty dollars?'

Craig didn't say anything.

'The buffet is just over there,' Jen said, pointing to a sign on their left. 'Let's get a table.'

Jen and Robert walked ahead to get a table. Andie was furious, but she wasn't going to make a scene. She'd talk to Craig later. By the time they got to the buffet, Jen had already paid for them.

'You didn't have to do that,' Andie said.

Jen smiled. 'Too late, it's already done. I'm still making up for Robert suggesting we come here.'

Craig waited until Jen and Robert had gone up to get food. 'We have to pay them back.'

Andie turned to look at him. 'With what? You just threw away our dinner money. And the money we need for tomorrow.'

Andie got up and went to the buffet. She didn't trust herself to say anymore. She was too angry.

Later that night, in their caravan, the time had come to stop being quiet.

'What were you thinking?' Andie said. 'How could you lose one hundred and fifty dollars?'

'I didn't think I'd lose. I thought I'd win some money we could use for the trip.'

'You know casinos always win.'

Craig didn't respond.

'And where did you get one hundred and fifty dollars? You were only supposed to have a third of that.'

And then Andie remembered thinking she should have had more money in her purse. She didn't need to ask the question. She could see it on his face.

'Why did you do it?'

Craig stayed silent.

'We're not going to bed until you answer my question.'

Craig still didn't say anything, but Andie wasn't going to let him get away with it, so she glared at him until he eventually gave in.

'Because I wanted to have fun at the casino.'

'How is losing money fun?'

Craig went silent again.

'We can't afford to lose one hundred and fifty dollars.'

Craig looked at her. 'It's not that much money.'

'Yes, it is. You don't know anything about our budget, do you?'

Craig looked sheepish. 'I didn't realise it was that tight.'

'Well, it is. We can't spend money like Jen and Robert do.'

The look on Craig's face turned from sheepish to resentment. 'I don't want to talk about their money.'

'Why? You've known all along they were going to have more money on this trip than us.'

'I didn't think it would stop us from doing things.'

Andie looked at him for a moment, trying to think of what they hadn't been able to do. Nothing came to mind. Until Robert decided he wanted to go to the casino. And had more than fifty dollars to gamble with.

Andie sighed. 'Let's go to bed. We've got a big day tomorrow.'

'Another island,' Craig said.

Andie turned back to look at him. 'Don't push it.'

Long after Craig had fallen asleep, Andie was still awake, thinking about what he'd done. It was so unlike him. Eventually, she gave up, got out of bed and went outside to sit by the caravan park pool. She couldn't understand why Craig didn't think it was a big deal. It wasn't so much that he'd taken the money without asking. It was that he'd taken it despite her telling him many times that they had to be careful with their money. Another thing he ignored her about.

The next morning, they boarded the ferry to Magnetic Island. They'd decided to take one car, and Craig volunteered to drive. Andie had hardly spoken to him since they'd woken up, still annoyed about what he'd done. She spent the ferry ride by herself, looking over the side at the ocean and back at the mainland, trying to change her frame of mind before they docked.

'So where to first?' Craig said as he drove off the ferry.

Jen smiled. 'Just to make you happy, Craig, we're starting with a walk.'

Craig grimaced but didn't say anything. Instead, he put the Forts Walk into the GPS and off they went. By the end of the day, they'd all enjoyed themselves, even Robert, who, for once, didn't complain about being in nature the whole time. Just some of the time. Which she wasn't including in the blog entry she'd just sat down to write.

Magnetic Island

Another lovely day on another lovely island. Magnetic Island this time. I think we'll all miss visiting islands when we leave Queensland.

Andie paused for a moment. Even Craig, with his whingeing about visiting another island, had eventually enjoyed himself. But she was still annoyed with him because of the money he'd taken.

We arrived at the World War II fort and were immediately taken with the views of the ocean. We stood mesmerised, watching the sun glisten on the cobalt water as far as the eye could see. It was stunning. And it was delightful spotting koalas in the gum trees scattered along the walk. As we stood there looking at the view and the bush that surrounded us, we all wondered what it would have been like during the war, when instead of taking in the view, the people here would have been looking for enemy ships.

After exploring the fort and the walking trails, we made a spontaneous decision to go and see the SS Adelaide. Jen found out about it when, on the ferry on the way over, she researched things to do. And the rest of us were glad she did. Where else could we see a sunken ship with trees growing from the deck, even though the ship was fully submerged?

As they'd glided across the sparkling blue sea, Andie thought for the first time what it would be like to own a boat. She'd watched the captain and how he skippered—the way he guided it from the dock to the wreck and back. He made it look effortless, and Andie wondered how long he'd been around boats. And how long it would take her to get to that level of confidence so she could make it look just as effortless. Craig had never shown any interest in boats, but maybe she could raise it.

After the tour to the SS Adelaide, we got back in the car and continued driving around the island. It's a very relaxed place, and it would have been nice to spend another day or two there. We came across a house with a large boulder almost butting into the side of it. It reminded us that wherever we go on this trip, there will be things we don't usually see.

And things that challenge us, Andie thought to herself. Or, more accurately, challenged her.

That night, they stayed at the caravan park. Craig and Robert stayed up drinking. Andie and Jen went to bed once they'd put the finishing touches on the blog. As much as Andie had originally thought it would be too time-consuming, she was beginning to realise how much she was enjoying writing each entry.

'Rise and shine,' Andie said the following day.

Craig rolled over and groaned.

'Time to get up.'

He didn't move, so Andie opened the curtain to let the sunlight stream in. Craig grabbed his pillow and shoved it over his head, yanking it down at the sides to cover his ears as well as his eyes.

'You can do that all you like. I know you can hear me, and I'm going to keep talking until you get up.'

Craig lifted the pillow off his head and looked at her. 'It's too early.'

'It's 8 am.'

'That's early.'

'No, it's not. You shouldn't have stayed up so late.'

'I was keeping Rob company.'

Andie hoped Craig hadn't called him that to his face. 'Is that what you call it?'

'Why do I have to get up now?'

'We're going up to the top of Castle Hill, and we need to go before it gets too hot.'

Craig sighed. 'All right. At least we can drive up there.'

Andie turned away from him and smiled. Oh no, she thought to herself. They weren't driving. They were walking. It was what she and Jen wanted to do. But she'd wait until they were all together to tell him so she and Jen could back each other up.

'No way,' Craig said fifteen minutes later.

Robert nodded in agreement. 'I'm too tired.'

Jen looked at both of them. 'Too bad. It's not negotiable.'

Andie nodded. 'You shouldn't have stayed up late drinking. Andie and I were sensible.'

Craig and Robert looked at each other and then at their wives. Then they got in the car for the drive to the base of Castle Hill.

'Come on,' Jen said, looking behind her. 'Pick up the pace.'

The women couldn't hear what the men said in response, but they could guess.

'This looks like a good place to take photos,' Jen said. 'Do you mind if we stop here for a minute?'

Andie shook her head. 'Take as many as you like. We probably should wait for them anyway.'

Andie watched as Craig and Robert walked towards them. They were still walking slowly and were both drinking from their water bottles.

'Do we have any more water,' Craig said as they got closer.

Andie shook her head.

'How much do you have left?'

'Not enough for you.'

'Isn't this view amazing,' Jen said, as she captured it with her phone.

'Yes,' Andie said. 'It was worth the walk.'

'No sure about that,' Craig said.

Andie ignored him, and they continued walking the rest of the way to the top. As Andie looked all around her, she could see the city. With its population of 179,000, it wasn't a sprawling metropolis, and it got Andie thinking more about moving to a smaller city. Maybe even a small town. Not too small though. She didn't want everyone to know everything about her and Craig. Or perhaps just her. On her own. Without Craig.

When they got back to their caravans, Craig and Robert sat down in chairs and didn't move except to get more water. Both said they were happy to stay where they were for the next few hours.

'If you two want to waste the rest of the day, that's your choice,' Jen said. 'But I'm not. Come on Andie, let's go.'

As Jen parked the car, Andie looked around her. The building in front of them wasn't that big. And as much as Jen enjoyed retail therapy, she was used to high-end stores and shopping centres in major cities. Not a regional centre where the choice of shops would be limited. Although, from the look on her face, she'd probably buy something anyway to cheer herself up. Even though Andie had noticed subtle, positive changes in how Jen and Robert interacted with each other, she could tell he was getting on Jen's nerves this afternoon.

Watching Jen shop wasn't how Andie wanted to spend the afternoon, but she didn't want to sit around the caravan park either. Or get into an argument with Craig about drinking so much the night before that he was squandering the afternoon.

The other alternative was to go off on her own. But then she'd be alone with her thoughts, and she didn't want that. Not with the earlier thought while they were walking up Castle Hill still fresh in her mind.

'Which way should we go?' Jen said as they walked in the door in the middle of the centre. 'Left?'

Andie was about to nod, but Jen was already off, focused on what she was there for.

An hour later, Jen had managed to buy two shirts, a dress and a pair of shorts, even though Andie thought they weren't her usual style.

'Don't buy too much more,' Andie teased. 'I've seen the wardrobe in your caravan.'

Jen laughed. 'You're right. And yes, I know I overpacked for this trip. Let's go and get a coffee.'

They found a table in a cafe and sat down.

'I'm glad we came here,' Jen said. 'And not just for the shopping. I needed to get away from Robert.'

Andie nodded. Even though she felt the same way about Craig, she didn't say anything.

'Why do they carry on like that?'

Andie shrugged. 'I don't know. Maybe they think they're still twenty.'

Jen drank the rest of her coffee in silence. She was thinking back to what Robert had said in Bowen. In all the years they'd been together, he'd never mentioned what had happened. Not even when the itinerary changed, and he knew they'd be heading there. Why did he shut her out when it came to his past?

They could have talked about it and come up with a way to make things easier for him. Jen could only assume he didn't want her help or support. She sighed to herself, wondering why she was surprised by that.

Across from her, Andie was finishing her coffee, and Jen was glad she'd let her have a few moments to herself. Andie had always known what to do. Jen wondered what Andie would say if she knew about the thoughts going through her mind while she sat opposite, so close and yet, so far away.

When they got back later that afternoon, their husbands were still sitting in the same spot. But now they were drinking.

'Seriously,' Jen said when she saw them.

Robert looked at her. 'What?'

'Are you going to do anything on this trip but sit around and drink?'

'We've done a lot so far. We're just having a relaxing afternoon.'

'And missing out on things you could be doing.'

'I'm happy doing this.'

Jen looked at Robert and then at Craig. 'We're going out to dinner tonight, so you better not drink too much.'

Andie turned to look at her. 'Are we? I thought we were staying here?'

'I've changed my mind. We're not sitting around here all night watching them drink.'

As soon as she'd finished speaking, she turned and walked to their caravan, shutting the door behind her. Andie didn't see her again until it was time to go. And when they did go out, Jen found a Thai restaurant that was BYO. Something she hadn't mentioned until after they were already inside.

'What sort of restaurant doesn't have wine,' Robert said as they sat down.

'This one,' Jen said. 'And we're staying.'

Over dinner, they talked about their journey the next day to Cairns. They planned to stay for a few days and visit Port Douglas, Mossman Gorge, and the Daintree River. This would be the furthest north they would go. Unfortunately, neither of their cars was set up for the heavy-duty four-wheel driving needed to get to Cape York.

The next morning, they packed up and got ready to go. Andie overheard Robert saying he was tired and asking Jen to drive.

'Why should I drive? You're the one who spent yesterday afternoon sitting around doing nothing. You should be well rested. And you snored for hours and kept me awake. There's nowhere else to go in the caravan.'

Robert didn't say anything. But he got in the driver's seat.

And Andie began to wonder if she'd been wrong in thinking that the positive changes between Jen and Robert were here to stay.

Five hours later, they were in Cairns. Even though they were now in the last month of autumn, it didn't feel cool. They were too far north for the usual cooler temperatures May brought back home. The look on Jen's face was no different than in Townsville. The rest of the day was spent walking around town, the two women walking in front of the men. And dinner that night was a quiet affair.

'Will we be there all day?' Robert said as they pulled up at the cable car terminal the following morning, ready to go up to Kuranda.

Jen nodded. 'Yes, we will. And it will be a great day.'

'Look at the queue,' Craig said.

Andie looked to where he was facing. 'Guess we're not the only ones who want to go to Kuranda.'

Jen started walking across the car park. 'It won't take long to get to the front.'

Andie and Craig looked at each other and then followed, Robert coming behind them.

Kuranda

Jen was right, and soon we were in the cable car heading up to Kuranda, a village in the rainforest on top of a mountain. The view on the way up was spectacular, with the ocean on one side and the rainforest on the other. At one point, we could see the train we would be catching later in the day winding its way down the mountain.

When we arrived, Jen knew the way to go, so we followed. The main street was more crowded than we thought it would be, being mid-week. But even with the number of people there, it still felt like a peaceful place.

For everyone but Robert, Andie thought to herself as she paused on the blog entry. As soon as they arrived, he started complaining that Kuranda was too artsy for him. But one look from Jen, and he stopped. The only time he'd said something was when Jen bought a small painting to hang up in the caravan, a touch of colour to add to the otherwise neutral interior. There's no room, Rob had said. The caravan has too many things in it already. But again, all it took was one look from Jen, and he stopped speaking.

By the end of the day, we'd walked all over town, looked in the shops and the galleries and had lunch at a charming pub—another enjoyable day on our adventure.

Accept that it wasn't, Andie thought, pausing again. Even though she'd enjoyed herself, especially the calm feeling she'd had while they'd been on top of the mountain, it hadn't been that way for everyone. More details she wouldn't be adding to the blog. But she replayed them in her head.

As they boarded the train, Jen had made it clear that the day hadn't been the same for her.

'He has no tolerance for anyone different to him,' she'd said. 'I don't want to live on a mountain wearing tie-dye clothes either, but if that's what someone wants to do, that's their choice.'

'I agree. But Robert's always been like that. At least in the time I've known him.'

Jen exhaled. 'Yes, I'm well aware of that. But I thought this trip would open his eyes.'

'Maybe it will. We've only just started.'

'I hope so.'

They'd sat in silence for the rest of the trip down the mountain. Andie had seen the guys were still talking, but they'd been too far away for her to hear what they were saying. By the time they'd got off the train, Jen was back to her usual self.

Andie pushed the conversation out of her mind, added Jen's photos, and then pressed publish. Anyone reading the blog would think they were having a wonderful time. All the time.

The next morning, they drove to Port Douglas. Andie used the time to mention the idea of getting a boat. Craig wasn't keen, so she dropped the subject. But only out loud. The boat stayed in her thoughts.

'What a beautiful stretch of highway,' Jen said after they arrived. 'Especially the section that hugged the coastline.'

Robert looked down at his phone. 'The Captain Cook Highway is one of the most picturesque in the country. It starts in Cairns and ends in Mossman, just north of here. That's something worth adding to your blog.'

Jen nodded. 'Yes, we'll add that. And I'm glad we get to see more of the highway when we go further north.'

We'll add it to the blog, Andie thought to herself, amused. I'll add the information to the blog is more like it. But, out loud, she said, 'Let's get set up. I'd like to look around town and then go for a swim.'

As they walked around the town, Andie couldn't help but notice how many international tourists there were.

Everywhere they strolled, she heard a cacophony of accents and wondered how they all decided to choose a destination in far north Queensland for their holiday, especially when they would have travelled a long way to get there.

'I can't believe how many good restaurants there are,' Robert said, interrupting Andie's thoughts. 'It will be hard to pick one for dinner tonight.'

Andie nodded but then thought that while the menus looked good, the prices did not. Clearly, this was a town that catered for the international tourists she saw everywhere.

'Speaking of food, should we have lunch?' Craig said.

Robert nodded. 'Good idea. Then we don't have to leave the beach early. Where shall we go?'

Andie looked around and saw a sign for a restaurant that had tapas and paella that was within their budget, and she started heading towards it before anyone else had a chance to say anything. If dinner was going to be expensive, they needed somewhere cheaper for lunch. Robert looked sceptical as they sat down, but he changed his mind once the food arrived. Or maybe it was the sangria that changed his mind. Andie wasn't sure.

'This isn't bad,' Craig said as he took a sip of the red wine and fruit punch.

'No, it's not,' Andie said. 'But we're going swimming, remember, so don't have too much.'

Port Douglas

We spent a lovely afternoon swimming in the warm, tropical North Queensland water. We also had an interesting conversation with a woman swimming near us. We're not sure where she was from, but by her accent, it was somewhere in Europe. She didn't understand why we all needed to swim in an area with a net around it. Further conversation highlighted the presence of stingers. This then required further explanation. That the most common form of stingers are jellyfish. And how much they hurt if you get stung by one. It was a good reminder that things that are commonplace to us are unfamiliar to others.

Following our afternoon of swimming, which we all enjoyed so much that we stayed in the water until our skin began to wrinkle, we headed back to the vans and got ready for our night on the town. Starting with dinner in a wonderful restaurant where we decided to be adventurous and order crocodile spring rolls. We ventured to one of the local establishments to witness an event that Craig suggested, and surprisingly, Jen and Robert were in favour of —cane toad racing. In Jen's explanation, this trip is all about doing things we wouldn't normally do. So that's how we found ourselves watching cane toads hopping across a circular ring as the patrons watched and cheered, hoping the toad they'd bet on would win. The true entertainment, though, was seeing the looks on the faces of the international tourists who had no idea what was going on. We just hoped they didn't go home and tell people that this was Australian culture.

As Andie typed, the same thought bubbled away in the back of her mind. One day she wanted to be doing what they were doing - visiting another country and seeing something she would never have dreamed of.

The next morning, they headed off to Mossman Gorge, not too far to the north. As they drove through cane fields and then through the town of Mossman, population 1937, Andie's mind went again to wondering what it would be like living in a small town. Maybe somewhere like this. Or perhaps a seaside town.

'Look at that,' Robert said, pointing at a sign as they got out of the car.

The sign said they shouldn't swim in the gorge, something they were all looking forward to doing.

'Don't worry,' Craig said. 'The sign doesn't say it's illegal.'

'I don't know,' Jen said.

'Let's go up and see what it's like,' Robert said.

They walked along timber boardwalks through lush rainforests until they reached the gorge. And there in front of them, no matter which direction they looked, people were swimming. Craig was the first to join them, followed by Robert, only a few seconds behind. Andie and Jen hopped into the water together, taking ages to psyche themselves up before plunging into the chilly water.

They were enjoying themselves until Robert decided to get his water bottle and slipped on the rocks on the way out.

'Guess that's why the sign is there,' Andie said.

She could hear Robert swearing and saying this is why he didn't like nature. She could also see the look on Jen's face as Robert swore. They had nothing to put over the cut, but luckily, one of the other swimmers had a first aid kit in her bag. Jen begrudgingly applied the band-aids, tired already of Robert's behaviour. But the quickest way to get him to stop complaining was for her to put the band-aids on and change the subject.

'Ok, that's enough now,' Jen said, standing up and looking directly at Robert, a stern look on her face. 'No more accidents. We've got a cruise on the Daintree River tomorrow that I'm really looking forward to.'

Andie shivered. It wasn't the boat cruise. It was the thought of the river being full of crocodiles. Hideous things. She'd happily miss seeing them, but then she'd miss the river.

Mossman

The gorge was stunning—crystal clear water, boulders smoothed by the flow, towering cliffs, all surrounded by rainforest, with white clouds above. As we floated in the water (freezing, I might add), it was hard to think of a more picturesque place. Although we've seen some already and will see many more before our trip is over, maybe that's not the correct statement. It was hard to leave, but eventually, we had to get out and head back to Port Douglas.

As Andie read what she'd written, she thought about the picturesque places they had yet to reach. What if she came across somewhere that was so appealing she really did want to move? What would that mean? For her and for Craig?

The following day, Andie wondered if she'd made the right decision about the river cruise. This thought came to her as she stood on the dock and looked at the boat they were about to board.

'It's very small,' she said to Jen.

'It's not that small. It can fit thirty people in it.'

Andie preferred something that could fit two hundred people and had high sides. She had this thought again the first time she spotted a crocodile. It was on the bank, watching the boat as it approached. The boat slowed beside the crocodile so people could take photos. Jen took several. Andie didn't take any. She spent the whole time hanging onto the sides of her seat, praying none of the people standing would start rocking the boat.

Why anyone would want to take photos of such a hideous creature, she didn't know. What she did know was there were many more she couldn't see lurking under the water, but she put that thought out of her mind and focussed on the beautiful scenery instead.

The Daintree was somewhere she'd always wanted to visit. The world's oldest rainforest and world heritage listed as well; it was an amazing place. The towering trees, the lush green canopy, and the calm, flowing river all untouched by human intervention. She'd even managed to put the crocodiles out of her mind. At least until lunch when she saw that crocodile was on the menu.

'Crocodile burger,' Craig said. 'Never tried one of those before.'

Andie looked at him. He wasn't usually a fan of any food that was out of the ordinary, although he had tried the crocodile spring rolls. It had been hard to pick the flavour because the spring roll had been deep-fried and covered in sauce. 'Are you going to try it?'

Craig nodded. 'Why not? Who else is going to try one?'

Jen and Robert looked at each other, and both shrugged.

'Ok,' Jen said. 'It's something different.'

Craig looked at Andie. 'Four then?'

Andie nodded. She wasn't sure about it, but if the others tried it and said it was delicious, she'd be disappointed that she hadn't been as adventurous with her lunch.

Ten minutes later, she was glad she'd made the decision. 'It tastes like a mix of chicken and fish.'

Jen nodded. 'I've been trying to pick what it tastes like, but that's it exactly.'

Robert put down his wine and nodded in agreement. It was the second one he'd had. When he'd ordered it, she'd noticed the look on Jen's face.

'So, tomorrow, we're heading inland again,' Craig said, grinning.

Robert turned away and looked out at the rainforest.

Their destination was Mt Isa, but at just over fourteen hours away, they talked about the journey and decided to break it, which is how they found themselves heading to Normanton the next day.

'Wow,' Jen said after they arrived. 'It's so dry.'

They looked around at the dusty main street and nodded in agreement, but after spending almost eight and a half hours in the car, they were glad they were staying the night. Normanton was only a small town, and it was a long way from anywhere, way up in the Gulf of Carpentaria. It was unlike any town they'd seen so far, even different to the small towns they'd stopped in when they went inland from Bowen.

From the look on Robert's face, he didn't seem impressed. 'Thank goodness we're leaving tomorrow.'

Jen turned to look at him. 'You could try and enjoy yourself while we're here.'

Robert shrugged. 'How? What is there to do?'

He was about to say something else but one look at Jen stopped him.

'What on earth is that?' she said, turning away from Robert and pointing to her right.

The others turned to where she was facing.

'That is hideous,' Andie said.

Jen started walking. 'I have to get a photo.'

'You can go on your own,' Andie said.

'No, come with me. You can be in the photo.'

Andie shook her head. 'No way. I'm staying here.'

So, three of them walked over to the monument.

Jen turned around when they got there and waved Andie over. 'It's only a replica. It's not real.'

Andie sighed and walked towards them and the monument of Krys the crocodile, a replica of the largest ever crocodile captured anywhere in the world, so she would have the details to add to the blog. She knew Jen would insist on including a photo. But as Andie looked at it, she decided the replica was bad enough. She couldn't imagine coming face to face with the 8.6 metre long beast in the wild.

'Stand in front of it,' Jen said.

Andie shook her head. 'I've walked over. That's enough.'

'I'll get in the photo,' Craig said.

Andie watched as not only did he walk right up to the replica but put his leg in its mouth and pretended to scream. Jen thought it was hilarious and took a few photos. Robert just shook his head and said he wasn't doing that. Andie wondered why Craig was so childish sometimes. But she knew she'd have to add that photo to the blog because he'd want their friends and family to see it.

'Let's go look at something else,' Craig said after the photos had been taken.

They continued to look around town and then had an early night so they would have plenty of sleep before the drive to Mt Isa.

Chapter Nine

There wasn't a lot to see on the way to Mt Isa. Just dry, dusty land and a highway that stretched for kilometres with no end in sight. Jen was happy she was driving because it gave her something to do. Just staring out the window for hours would have driven her crazy. That wasn't something that Robert had to worry about, as he'd fallen asleep not long after they'd left Normanton. Given the condition of the road and the fact that it was long and straight, and it would be easy to lose concentration, she would have preferred he was awake and talking to her. But when she mentioned that as they started off, he said she'd be fine and rested his head against the seat. He only woke up when she pulled over and told him it was his turn to drive.

'What's that?' Jen said, looking to her left as they got out of the cars after arriving in town.

'It must be part of the mine,' Craig said.

Robert grimaced. 'Great, another town full of miners.'

Jen turned to look at him. 'Just because those two in Collinsville weren't very nice doesn't mean all miners are like that.'

Robert didn't look convinced.

'There's the visitors centre,' Andie said. 'Let's go and see what they suggest we visit while we're here.'

'There's a mine that tourists can look at,' Jen said once they were inside.

Robert didn't even look up before saying no.

'Why not?' Craig said. 'It would be interesting.'

Robert stayed silent but shook his head. A dark look crossed Jen's face, and she was about to say something when Andie spoke up. The visitor centre wasn't the place for Jen and Robert to get into an argument.

'We should go to the City Lookout,' Andie said. 'It says here that you can see the whole town from up there.'

Jen nodded, though her words came out stilted. 'That sounds nice, and it will be a good place to get photos.'

At least the photos will keep her occupied, Andie thought to herself. They hadn't even left Queensland, and she'd already lost count of how many photos Jen had taken. The blog only needed so many. But if taking photos kept her happy, then Andie wasn't going to say anything.

'You'll want to take photos of this too,' Andie said.

Jen walked over to where Andie was and looked at what she'd been reading.

'An underground hospital sounds fascinating.'

'It is.'

Andie and Jen turned around at the sound of the voice to see the woman who worked in the visitors' centre walk towards them.

'Back in 1942, people were concerned about the Japanese bombing the town, so they wanted to move the hospital somewhere safe.'

'That makes sense,' Jen said.

The woman nodded. 'And there were plenty of miners and equipment to make the move.'

'I'm glad it's been preserved so we can still see it,' Jen said.

She tried to imagine what it would have been like, being underground, the doctors and nurses checking on their patients lying in their beds, worried all the time that a bomb might drop from a Japanese plane. And the patients, some of them unable to move. How did they feel knowing there was a chance they could be bombed? It made what Jen had been feeling towards Robert seem unimportant in comparison.

But still, her unhappiness niggled. If it was unhappiness. Maybe she was just stuck in a rut, one she hoped this trip would drag her out of. The more she thought about herself, Robert, and their life together, the more confused she became. If only someone would give her the answer she was looking for.

'I enjoyed this afternoon,' Craig said, looking down over the city as the sun began to fade from the sky.

Jen nodded. 'Me too. Especially the underground hospital. That was fascinating.'

Andie nodded too. 'I liked that as well.'

They turned to look at Robert, but he didn't say anything.

'Anything you liked about today?' Jen said, prompting him.

Robert shrugged. 'Nothing stood out.'

'What?' Craig said. 'How can you say that?'

'It's just not my thing.'

'What isn't?'

'These outback places.'

'But that's half the trip.'

'Then I guess I'll only enjoy the other half of the trip.'

Craig watched as Robert walked to the other side of the lookout and then turned to Jen.

'What's up with him?'

Jen shrugged. 'Who knows?'

Andie could tell by the look on her face that she couldn't be bothered to find out either. She hoped they'd be all right.

Ironic, she thought, given what had been going through her mind. Craig looked like he was going to say something else, but before any words came out, he changed his mind.

Robert's mood only improved when they got to dinner.

'This looks ok,' he said, as he looked around the restaurant. 'The menu isn't bad either.'

'What did you expect?' Craig said.

'You never know in these places.'

Andie watched him as he concentrated on what he was going to order. From here, they were only heading further into the outback. What was he going to be like? She was still thinking about that when she saw him smile. And then she realised it was because he was reading the wine list. When the wine arrived, he smiled again. A detail Andie left out of the blog.

Mt Isa

We met a lovely woman at the visitors' centre who gave us lots of great information. As well as visiting the underground hospital, which was amazing, we spent the rest of the day walking around town, seeing the sites she'd mentioned, one of which was a very interesting sign.

As you can see by the photo below (one of the many Jen took!), the sign caused us all to smile. None of us expected to see a sign informing us that it was 15,150 kilometres from Mt Isa to London. Or another one that told us it was 16,173 kilometres to New York. We assumed the signs were there for trivia as I couldn't imagine flights from those destinations starting to land at Mt Isa Airport.

We finished the day at the City Lookout on the recommendation of the visitors' centre volunteer. Not long after we got there, the sun began to set, casting a yellow-orange glow across the town. The same colour glow lit up the night sky as they turned on the lights at the mine.

As Jen looked over Andie's shoulder at what had been written, she tried not to think about the other sites they could have seen. The ones Robert vetoed. He'd said they're all about mining, and that was the end of the conversation. They could have started the conversation again, but none of them had the energy to try and change Robert's mind. He had agreed to go to the City Lookout, although Jen knew it was because he was already thinking about the dinner they'd be going to after. He'd already got them to agree to go somewhere decent, which Jen also knew was code that wherever they went needed to have a wine list. As it turned out, the place he picked did.

The next morning, Robert had gone back to the way he'd been before dinner the previous evening. As Jen looked at him, she tried to decide whether it was because he wasn't looking forward to the journey that day or because of the headache he must have after the wine he'd drunk. She was leaning towards the latter, although he'd never admit it.

Mt Isa to Tennant Creek

This morning, we headed off to Camooweal early. It took us almost three hours to get there, and we still needed to drive another five and a half hours to get to today's destination— Tennant Creek. We had a brief stop in Camooweal, getting out to stretch our legs before continuing. Like the day before, there wasn't a lot to look at during the drive, but we wanted to cross the Queensland and Northern Territory border, so we kept going until we pulled up in Tennant Creek.

As Andie added the start of that day's entry while waiting for the others to get ready, she thought back to their arrival late that afternoon. Robert's mood hadn't improved during the drive, so they ignored him. The only thing that put a smile on his face was their plan to head out for dinner. That was until they arrived at the pub, which turned out to be like the one in Collinsville. His smile soon disappeared.

When they finished dinner, Craig wanted to play pool. Robert said no, but she and Jen said they'd take turns playing. Robert stayed at the table, a look of irritation extending across his face. He didn't move until his drink ran out. That's when he got up and walked to the bar. As he leant on the bar waiting, a man staggered up, stumbled, and fell into him.

Robert turned to look at him. 'Careful.'

'What do you mean? You're the one who bumped me. You owe me a drink.'

Robert shook his head. 'You fell into me. I don't owe you anything.'

'I said, you owe me a drink.'

Robert turned back to the bar and ignored him.

'Listen, mate. Just cause you're not from around here, you look like a city bloke to me, doesn't mean you can treat me like that.'

Before Robert could say anything, the barman leaned over and told the guy to shut up.

'I saw you. You fell into him. He did nothing wrong.'

'Stay out of it.'

'I won't, and if you don't stop, I'll throw you out. You've had enough anyway.'

The man looked at the barman and scowled. He started to turn away, but before he moved, he pushed Robert and called him a wanker.

'That's it,' the barman said. 'Get out.'

'Who's going to make me?'

'I will.'

The man turned around to see Craig standing behind him, the difference in their builds evident to anyone watching. The man looked Craig up and down and was about to say something but then thought better of it. He stood his ground though. Until Craig took a step closer, then he turned and walked out.

Craig went back to the pool table, and none of them saw Robert walk outside. He didn't walk far before he saw the man leaning against the corner of the building. Robert walked up behind him, pushed him, so he fell, and then walked back inside. He could hear the man swearing and calling out, but the barman wouldn't let him back in. Eventually, the barman had enough and told one of the other patrons to take the man home and put him to bed.

No one saw Robert smile. He'd never done anything like that before. But after Collinsville, he wasn't letting anyone get away with treating him like that again.

The next morning, Robert was in a good mood, almost cheerful, even though they had a five-hour drive to Alice Springs. And he was still in a good mood when they arrived.

'What's with him this morning?' Craig asked.

Jen shrugged. 'No idea. But I'm not questioning it.'

Then she went back to her phone and continued searching for things to do. After a moment or two, she found something.

'Has anyone ever heard of a dry river regatta?'

The others shook their heads.

'The Henley-on-Todd Regatta. 'Boats' are made of metal frames and hung with banners, and the 'crews' run their boats in races through the hot sand. It is the only dry river regatta in the world.'

'I'd love to see that,' Craig said.

'Me too,' Jen said as she kept reading. 'Damn. It's the wrong time of year.'

Andie smiled. 'Guess we'll have to make do with Uluru.'

Jen smiled too. 'I suppose that will have to do.'

They both laughed. Uluru had been one of the must-see places when they'd been planning the trip.

'That's not until tomorrow though,' Craig said. 'What shall we do this afternoon?'

'There's plenty to look at around town,' Jen said, consulting her phone again. 'And maybe tomorrow morning, before we head off, we could go hot air ballooning.'

Craig shook his head. 'No way am I going up in one of those things.'

'Oh, that's right,' Robert said. 'You don't like heights.'

Craig turned to look at him. 'Nothing wrong with that. Lots of people don't like heights.'

Robert shrugged. 'Didn't say there was anything wrong with it. I just think it would be a great thing to do.'

Jen nodded. 'Me too. The view would be magical.'

'Why don't you two go?' Andie said. 'You can take lots of photos and show us.'

Jen laughed. 'There'll definitely be lots of photos. Why don't you come with us though? You're not afraid of heights.'

Craig interrupted her before she had a chance to say anything else. 'I'm not afraid. I just don't like heights.'

'Stay behind then,' Robert said. 'I'm sure Andie will be happy to come with us.'

Andie shook her head. 'I don't need to go. I'll stay here.'

'You shouldn't miss out,' Craig said. 'I'll go.'

As he said the words, she knew he didn't mean it, so she shook her head again, even though she did want to go. But she also didn't want to deal with Craig's reaction if she went. To mask her disappointment, she told herself it wasn't in the budget anyway.

The next morning, Jen knocked on the door of Andie and Craig's caravan. It was still dark outside.

Andie opened the door. 'What's wrong?'

Jen smiled. 'Nothing. But we'll miss the sunrise if we don't go now.'

'What are you talking about?'

'I've bought four tickets for the hot air balloon. Craig said yesterday that he'd go.'

'You shouldn't have done that. How much do we owe you?'

'Nothing. It's my treat. Now, let's go.'

Andie shut the door and turned to look at Craig. 'Are you going to be ok going up?'

He nodded. 'Of course.'

As she watched his face, she knew he was lying. And the fact that he didn't mention anything about Jen paying for the tickets let her know how worried he was. But she knew that if

Robert was going up, so was he. She also knew that Jen wouldn't take any money for the tickets.

'Morning, everyone,' the pilot said when they arrived. 'It's a beautiful day for a balloon ride.'

'Not sure about that,' Craig said under his breath so only Andie could hear.

The pilot spent a few minutes going through the safety instructions and telling them about their trip. When he was done, he told them to jump on board.

'It's not long until sunrise, so we need to be up there so you can get the best view.'

Robert and Jen got on first. Andie went next. Craig was last and walked to the basket much slower than he usually did. Once inside, he stood in the middle.

'You need to be at the side to distribute the weight evenly,' the pilot said. 'And hold on as we go up in case it's a bit bumpy.'

From the look on Craig's face, Andie wondered if he'd climb back out of the basket. But he did as the pilot asked, although he didn't turn around and look out and over the side, instead staring at the floor of the basket. There was nothing to worry about as the balloon glided up from the ground.

'Not long now,' the pilot said when they were up in the air.

Five minutes after the pilot said those words, the sun came up, Andie wrote in the Alice Springs blog entry afterwards. *Then none of us spoke. We were too mesmerised by the view. It was breathtaking. The early morning light shone over the desert and the colours that came with it. As far as we could see, there was beauty. Even Craig forgot for a moment that he didn't like heights and actually let go of the basket long enough to take a photo on his phone.*

He probably wouldn't like that Andie included that, but she didn't care.

Jen started taking photos ever since the balloon began to rise. I just looked at the view, feeling at peace. No matter what happened during or after the trip, we will all remember this moment.

The next morning, they were up early to start their journey to Uluru. As they drove through the desert, Andie looked out at the barren landscape. No people, no buildings, and no sign of human intervention anywhere. She turned the air conditioning off and wound down the window to let in the desert air. Craig whinged about it for a few moments but then started to enjoy the feel of the breeze. In the back seat, neither Jen nor Robert said anything.

Because they weren't taking the caravans, they'd decided to go in one car. In the rear vision mirror, Andie saw Jen staring straight ahead and Robert looking out the window. Neither of them had spoken since they'd left.

Jen knew that Andie was aware of how annoyed she was with Robert, but she couldn't be bothered hiding it. Why did he have to drink so much last night? Like he had on so many other nights. This was meant to be an adventure, something they'd remember for the rest of their lives. Not a drinking holiday around Australia.

As they continued through the desert, Jen looked at the desolate landscape. It suited her mood perfectly. But then, when they were almost at their destination, Robert reached across the backseat and took hold of her hand, silently apologising at the same time. Maybe it wasn't too late, Jen thought to herself.

Uluru

As we drove down the highway, we were surrounded by nothingness. That was until we arrived at our destination. There were so many cars and buses, we were lucky to find a car park. It wasn't as close as we would have liked, but we were so taken by the sight of 'The Rock' that we didn't mind.

It was amazing, as evidenced by the photos below that Jen took. We stayed where we were, unable to do anything but stare. Eventually, we moved and headed off, walking around the base. The crowd swallowed us up as we walked, surrounded by so many people that it felt like we were in a city. It was such a magical place that even Craig didn't complain about the walk. We wanted to stay longer but needed to check in at our accommodation.

As they pulled into the car park, Andie closed the laptop and hopped out of the car, looking at the resort as she did. Inside, taking a few deep breaths, she handed over her credit card. She was about to pay for a more expensive room than expected, and she would soon be paying for an overpriced lunch. She'd been managing their budget carefully, and hopefully, this wouldn't impact their activities for the rest of the week. She'd have to talk to Craig though. He was the one who'd agreed straight away to stay at the resort and to include lunch as well as dinner. Andie wasn't surprised that he'd said it the same day Jen had bought the tickets for the hot air balloon ride.

An hour later, Andie was well aware that she'd been right about the cost of lunch, although considering how delicious the food was, she was determined to push that thought out of her mind. She watched Jen and Robert eat the prawns they'd ordered and wondered where they had come from. They were in the middle of the country, as far as you could get from the ocean. Craig wanted to order prawns too, but she shook her head at him when no one else was looking. For once, he didn't push the point.

We spent the rest of the day at the resort, swimming in the pool and relaxing until it was time to head back to Uluru for the sunset. When we arrived, the car parking situation was worse than it had been earlier. We eventually found a spot, which we were grateful for as we wanted to stay until the sun disappeared completely from the sky above us.

As we looked around, we couldn't believe the difference between now and only a few hours earlier. We'd heard that the rock changed colour at sunset, and now we were looking at it, we could see that it really did—different shades of orange, red and brown. As you can see below, Jen took so many photos that I had to tell her to put down her camera and look at it with her eyes, not through a lens. I'm glad she took so many, though. I think these photos will be ones that we will look at for a long time to come, although all of us are sure we will never forget the sight in front of us.

The atmosphere also had an impact on Robert and Jen. Andie watched out the corner of her eye as Robert put his arms around her, pulling her closer. Craig stood apart from Andie and stayed that way until it was time to get back in the car. Andie decided to leave that detail out as she was adding the entry later that evening.

Now for some information about where we were. At 348 metres high, it is one of the largest monoliths in the world. And with its perimeter of 9.4 kilometres, it dominates the surrounding landscape. We could see why it's visited by around 300,000 people every year, even though it's in a very remote location, with Alice Springs being 450 kilometres away. It is around 550 million years old, and tourists have been heading there since the late 1930s.

Andie finished typing and put her laptop away, not sure her words did the place justice. But the way she was feeling about Craig and their marriage, it was all she could manage. If even a place as magical as this didn't provide some moments of closeness between them, she realised that nothing would.

The following day they were back on the highway and heading north. They had a long drive ahead to get to Katherine.

That was until Robert checked the map. 'Change of plans.'

'Why?' Craig said.

'The distance between here and Katherine is 1643 kilometres.'

'Not doing that in a day.'

'How long would it take to drive?' Jen said.

Robert looked at the map again. 'Just over twenty hours.'

'Back to Alice Springs it is then,' Andie said as she unlocked the driver's door.

As they got in the car, Andie couldn't help thinking about what Robert had said. It was unlike him not to have the next part of their drive organised well in advance. Clearly, the closeness that he and Jen had experienced at Uluru had carried on later into the night.

'It's still too far to get from Alice to Katherine in a day, so we'll have to stop somewhere else,' Craig said as they drove through the desert.

Robert consulted the map but didn't look pleased by what he found. 'It looks like our only option is to drive from Alice Springs to Tennant Creek and stay there again.'

'It will be fine,' Jen said. 'We'll avoid the pub.'

'What are the distances?' Andie asked.

'It's 508 kilometres from Alice to Tennant and then 674 kilometres from Tennant to Katherine,' Robert said.

'That's two big days,' Andie said. 'Anywhere we can stop on the way, at least to get out of the cars for a while?'

Robert did some more research on his phone. 'Here's something. About 107 kilometres south of Katherine is a place called Mataranka.'

'What's there?' Craig said.

'Hot springs.'

'I'll be in that,' Jen said.

Andie nodded in agreement. 'Sounds lovely.'

So that's how they found themselves adding Mataranka to the itinerary.

That night in Tennant Creek, they had a BBQ at the caravan park and didn't go anywhere. When they pulled up at the petrol station, Robert saw the man who had hassled him. He looked right at Robert but didn't seem to recognise him. Even so, Robert was the one who suggested the BBQ.

The following morning, they headed off and by the time they arrived in Mataranka, they were all ready for the hot springs.

After the long and boring drive, we arrived at
Mataranka, in the middle of nowhere, surrounded by desert but,
in the middle, an oasis with hot springs. We spent a few hours
exploring and floating in the pools, not wanting to get out and
continue the drive north, but eventually, we had to. But not
before we remembered why the name sounded familiar.
Mataranka is the setting for the novel 'We of the Never Never'
by Jeannie Gunn.

Like yesterday, Jen and Robert were close, floating together, their arms around each other at times. Andie had tried to put her arm around Craig, but he'd shrugged it off. So, as he was drying off, Andie pulled out her laptop and pretended to be focused solely on the blog.

Arriving in Katherine, they were all tired after the drive, even with the break in the middle, and they went to bed early in preparation for the early start the next day. They'd booked a boat trip on Katherine Gorge, which they were all looking forward to.

That was, until the following morning, when they were seated in the boat, and Jen mentioned that crocodiles could be found in the gorge.

Andie turned to look at her. 'I notice you didn't tell me until now.'

'You might not have come along if I'd told you earlier.'

Andie shuddered. 'I hope I don't see any.'

'It could be worse,' Jen said. 'We could try and talk you into doing the crocodile cruise on the Adelaide River.'

Andie shook her head. 'No way.'

Jen laughed. 'It might be fun.'

Andie shook her head. 'I can't see how a river well known for its high concentration of saltwater crocodiles, a lot of whom jump vertically out of the water when the boats come along, could be an enjoyable day out.'

But even with her misgivings, the gorge was beautiful, and Andie had enjoyed the boat cruise. It had even pushed the thoughts of Craig out of her mind. The next day they were heading off to Kakadu, and she was looking forward to that, hoping the beauty of the place would distract her from her thoughts as well. But for now, she had another blog entry to do before they had dinner.

Katherine Gorge

As we looked at the rocks that form the gorge, we were surprised to see how high the water level rises in the wet season. When the rains come between November and April, the water rises to around 12 metres. In the dry season, the water level is only around 1.8 metres. Like many places in the Northern

203

Territory, the scenery at Katherine Gorge is stunning, with waterfalls, rock pools, and untouched wilderness. And at sunrise and sunset, the rocks in the gorge turn all shades of mauve and red. And even though the gorge is freshwater, saltwater crocodiles still inhabit it.

As she typed the last point, Andie was glad she hadn't seen any. No one else was bothered by them, but they filled Andie with dread. Creatures with no interest in you other than taking your life and your chance of new experiences and new memories. Or new people.

Kakadu and Darwin

Apologies for not updating the blog for the past two days. We've been having too much fun!

Which was mostly true. Craig had been more distant than usual, but Andie hadn't had the energy to question him. Her thoughts turned back to the idea that he was having a mid-life crisis. It would explain a lot.

Kakadu was stunning. The scenery was beautiful, as was the Aboriginal art. I was even persuaded to swim in a few water holes after being convinced there were no crocodiles in the vicinity. Even Robert enjoyed himself, which was great to see. It seems like he is finally getting into nature. Kakadu is 151 kilometres south of Darwin. It covers 20,000 square kilometres, so there was no way we could see all of it, but we spent the day walking through pristine bushland, looking at rock art and swimming in rockpools beneath waterfalls.

From there, it was off to Darwin, which has beautiful weather in these first few days of June, considering it's supposedly the beginning of winter.

We stumbled across Mindil Beach and discovered the markets. All along the beachfront were rows of market stalls and food trucks. All around them, people had set up chairs and tables and treated the area as one big outdoor restaurant, with each food truck forming part of the menu. The only problem was, with so many to choose from, it was hard to narrow down what we wanted. Yet, it all looked so good. After we had finally decided, we joined the other diners and ate while we watched the sunset over Mindil Beach and the Timor Sea.

The next day, we started our exploration of the city in earnest, taking in the city centre and waterfront precinct. The city centre provided our next surprise as we came across Crocosaurus Cove, the only place in Australia where you can dive with crocodiles. But with a name like the Cage of Death experience, there was no way I was doing that. That, plus my dislike of crocodiles. But the others still wanted to visit

Crocodylus Park, located fifteen minutes outside Darwin. The park is packed with crocodiles of all sizes in different pens. When we got to the feeding pen, I was happy to watch from a distance as the employees stood inside the enclosure, putting dead chickens on the edge of the water hole to entice the crocs outs. And the pen where the crocodiles 'jump' to get food, was another I stayed well back from. I can't wait until we leave the north and no longer have to hear the word 'crocodile'!

From there, we headed to the Northern Territory Museum and Art Gallery, where our third surprise awaited. The Cyclone Tracy exhibit is not just a static display. It has a section where you enter a room, the door is shut behind you, and the lights are turned off. As you stand in the pitch-black room, the noise starts—the sound of the cyclone as it tears across the city. Cyclone Tracy occurred on Christmas Eve, 1974. It was a category four, and it flattened most of the city. It's the worst cyclone Darwin has ever had, and if the feeling of being in that dark room with the sound of the winds and flying debris was even a tenth of what it was actually like, it must have been terrifying.

Our last stop exploring Darwin was the Defence of Darwin Experience, which has visual, aural and multimedia displays depicting what happened in the city during World War II. Some of the guns used to defend Darwin are still there, as is a display of military equipment, including machinery, medals and

uniforms. There is also a short movie that depicts the bombing of
Darwin by the Japanese that is very interesting to watch.

Andie read what she'd typed, then hit publish. She felt
tired today, more so than any other day recently. All she wanted
to do was go back to Mindil Beach and watch the sunset. But
Craig and Robert wanted to go to the casino, which was near the
beach. But, if Andie was sitting by the water, she couldn't keep
an eye on Craig and his spending.

It was their last night in Darwin. Tomorrow they'd be
heading west, crossing the border into Western Australia, where
their first stop would be the town of Kununurra.

Chapter Ten

Andie pointed across the road to the pub's outdoor terrace. 'Isn't that Eric?'

Jen turned to look where she was pointing and nodded as a shiver ran down her spine. 'That's someone I never wanted to see again.'

'What's he doing here?'

'No idea. I haven't seen or heard from him in years.'

'Breaking up with him was one of the best decisions you ever made.'

Jen shuddered. 'I should have done it a long time before I did.'

'You didn't know what he was truly like. He was very charming at first.'

'That should have been a clue. No guy is ever that charming without there being something wrong. He treated me like a princess until we moved in together. Once that happened, I was no longer important to him.'

'I think he's seen us.'

Jen looked across the road, and Eric was staring at them. Then he waved. 'Let's go. I don't want him walking over.'

As they walked off, Andie's thoughts went back to when Jen and Eric were together. Charming was definitely the right word. He charmed everyone he came across, Andie included. Craig never liked him, but at the time, Andie thought it was because Eric tended to believe he was better than everyone else. And whenever Craig talked to him, he always came away feeling like he was second best. It turned out that Craig was right not to like him.

Six months after moving in together, Jen discovered that he regularly went through her phone and emails. When she confronted him, he lied and said she was making it all up, that she was overreacting, even though she'd caught him doing it. She kept asking until he finally said he just wanted to know where she was going and what she was doing. This was unacceptable for Jen, who'd never looked at a single message on his phone. He promised he'd stop but not long after, she caught him again. That was the last straw. When she told him, any pretence of being charming went out the window. That's when she knew it was time to go. It was a decision he didn't agree with, and he'd become nastier by the day. Not long after Jen moved out, she heard a noise one day and looked up to see Eric staring through the window of her house, watching her as she ate dinner. She kept her calm and asked him to leave, and he never came back. But he continued to call and text her constantly. She ignored the calls and the texts, and eventually, they stopped. Not long after, she met Robert.

'I can't believe we've seen him,' Jen said.

'Are you going to tell Robert?'

Jen shook her head. 'Just seeing him was enough. I don't want to mention his name again.'

But as much as she would have liked that to be the case, it didn't turn out that way. That night, as they ate dinner in one of the local restaurants, Eric walked in and sat at a nearby table. He kept looking over at them but didn't get up.

'Isn't that your psycho ex?' Craig said.

Andie punched him lightly in the arm. 'Not so loud.'

Craig shrugged. 'We all know he's crazy.'

'So, let's not do anything to provoke him.'

'Or make him come over,' Jen said.

'He wouldn't dare,' Robert said.

Robert was right. He didn't come over. But the following day, they saw him again as they ate breakfast outside their caravans. He was standing outside the shop at the entrance to the park.

'I know Kununurra isn't a big town, but three times in two days is odd,' Andie said.

They thought no more about it as they didn't see him again, and the following day, they left for Broome at 5 am. It was a ten-and-a-half-hour drive, and even though it was winter, the days were still hot, and there was still a bite in the sun as it shone through the windscreens. They drove for hours without seeing anything and stopped briefly now and then, just long enough to stretch their legs.

'I couldn't imagine living anywhere this remote,' Andie said as the kilometres behind them became further than those in front of them.

Craig nodded in agreement. 'I couldn't either. I guess that's why there are not many people out here.'

'It was peculiar seeing Eric after all these years. And a bit creepy how he ended up in places we happened to be. Do you think it's a coincidence?'

'Must have been. But don't worry about it now. We've left Kununurra, and we'll never see him again.'

Andie stared out the window and hoped Craig was right. She was still thinking that an hour later when they saw the welcome to Broome sign.

'From what we've seen so far, this looks like a lovely town,' Andie said. 'I'm glad we're spending a couple of days here.'

Craig nodded. 'So am I. And it will be good not to be in the car for hours on end.'

Robert nodded too. 'That last hour before we got here was hard.'

Jen shivered. 'I don't care how long we were in the car. I'm just glad to be far away from Eric.'

Andie reached over and squeezed Jen's hand. 'Did it bother you that much?'

Jen nodded. 'Just something about the way he looked at me. It was unsettling.'

'Well, he's nowhere near us now,' Robert said. 'So, let's concentrate on what we're going to do while we're here. I've made a list.'

Craig turned to look at him. 'Of course you have.'

'It doesn't hurt to be prepared,' Robert said. 'If we're not, we'll miss things we plan to see.'

'You might also miss things because the planned itinerary is so full that it doesn't leave time to explore. You don't know what you might find.'

'You probably won't find anything. If it's worth seeing, then there will be some mention of it online by other travellers. Now, this is what I've found.'

'I hope a camel ride on Cable Beach is on the list,' Craig said before Robert had a chance to say anything else.

Robert nodded. 'It's at the top. I thought we could do that tomorrow afternoon at sunset.'

'Isn't the oldest outdoor movie theatre here as well?' Craig interrupted again before Robert could continue.

Robert nodded. 'Also on the list. Which I'll go through if you let me finish.'

As Robert rattled off the rest of the things he'd planned for them to do, Andie looked at Craig out of the corner of her eye. He was annoyed and not hiding it. Not that Robert noticed. He was too busy being their tour guide. Jen didn't seem to notice either, and she was usually good at picking up on things like that. Her mind really was elsewhere. Was there something about Eric that Jen hadn't told her? Later that night, she asked.

Jen sighed. 'He told me once that if I ever left him, he'd hurt me.'

'What do you mean hurt?'

'Physically.'

'Why didn't you tell me?'

'Because he was drunk when he said it, so I just ignored it. And apart from that night, he looked in my window, I haven't seen him since we broke up.'

'But you've remembered now.'

'It was the way he looked at me. Like he'd remembered what he'd said and knew I'd remembered it too.'

'We're in a different town, a long way from where we saw him. I'm sure there's nothing to worry about.'

As Andie went to bed that night, she hoped she was right.

Over the next few days, they went sightseeing to canyons, waterfalls and beaches and walked around town, taking in everything on Robert's list. They even found time to detour and visit the historical museum. Even though Craig wasn't all that interested in going, it made him happy that they were doing something that wasn't on the list.

Broome

Riding a camel on Cable Beach at sunset was always part of the plan. The beach itself is beautiful, the camels not so much. They're adorable to look at, but I spent the ride hanging on for dear life. An image of me dangling from the side, foot stuck in the stirrups while trying to get my arms around the camel's neck to stay on, was vivid in my mind. Thankfully, Jen didn't capture that in a photo!

Cable Beach is 22 kilometres long, meandering along the turquoise-blue water of the Indian Ocean. Our research told us it was named for the telegraph cable laid between Broome and Java in 1889.

Another must-see in Broome is the Staircase to the Moon, which only occurs when there is a full moon, and the tide is out at Roebuck Bay. When the moonlight shines down, it looks like a staircase is rising from the water up to the moon. It's one of the most popular things tourists do while in the area.

Andie looked once more at the words, added some of Jen's photos then clicked Save. That was enough for now. Even though the more she wrote, the more she enjoyed it, she hadn't been able to concentrate the past few days.

On the last night in Broome, they went to the world's oldest outdoor picture garden to watch a movie. Sitting five rows behind them was Eric.

'What the hell?' Robert said. 'I don't like this at all.'

'It's just a coincidence,' Jen said. 'It has to be.'

'We're ten and a half hours away from where we saw him,' Craig said.

'Maybe he's travelling for work,' Andie said, knowing that even as she said it, she didn't believe it.

Robert shook his head. 'Something isn't right.'

Jen moved her chair closer to Robert's, reached over and took hold of his hand.

Andie moved her chair closer to Craig's. 'Should we leave?'

Craig shook his head. 'We're not giving him the satisfaction of making us leave the movie. Just ignore him.'

Andie reached over and squeezed Jen's other hand. 'Do you want to go?'

She shook her head. 'Craig's right. We can't let him change our plans. I don't want him to realise how scared I am right now.'

Robert pulled her closer. 'I won't let him anywhere near you.'

Craig nodded in agreement. 'Me either.'

So, they stayed and watched the movie, although none of them took much of it in. When they got up to leave, Eric stopped them in the walkway.

'What a surprise seeing you here.'

'Is it?' Robert said.

Eric smiled. 'I'm not sure what you mean.'

'You know very well what I mean. Are you following us?'

'Why would I do that?'

'I don't know. You tell me.'

Eric didn't respond. He just smiled.

Beside her, Andie could see Craig take a few steps forward so he was next to Robert. And in front of Jen.

Eric stood his ground. 'I thought it might be nice to catch up with Jen again.'

Robert crossed his arms. 'She doesn't want to catch up with you.'

'I'm sure she does. For old times' sake.'

Jen spoke for the first time. 'I made it clear when we broke up that I never wanted to see you again.'

'You just said that because you were acting out at losing the best thing in your life.'

Craig snorted. 'You've got to be joking. I remember you very well. You're a waste of space.'

Eric took a step closer to them. 'Watch what you say.'

'I'll say whatever I like. There are two of us and one of you. What are you going to do about it?'

Eric didn't say anything. He just stared at them. Eventually, he turned around and left.

'What an arsehole,' Craig said.

Robert put his arm around Jen. 'You're not going anywhere without me until we leave town. If he was stupid enough to come up to you when we were all here, I don't think he'd hesitate to come up to you if you were on your own.'

Jen didn't say anything. She just stared in the direction that Eric had gone. But as he walked away, she couldn't help but feel something different for Robert. He might drive her crazy at times, so much so that she doubted their future together, but the way he'd stepped up caused her to re-evaluate all she'd been feeling.

The next day, they left earlier than they had planned. In the car, Andie turned to Craig. 'It's not a coincidence, is it?'

Craig shook his head. 'Not anymore.'

'But that has to be the last time we see him.'

'We said that in Kununurra. Not that I'd say that to Jen. We need to keep a watch from now on.'

Andie continued to look at him while he drove.

'I didn't know you were that interested in my driving,' he said after a while.

Andie turned back to look out the windscreen. She'd been thinking that he'd become the old Craig again. Maybe not everything was exactly as she wanted it to be, but maybe what she had was enough. Or perhaps it wasn't. She didn't know anymore.

Four hours later, they pulled over at a rest area. They still had two hours to go to Port Hedland, and they could have pushed through, but Andie and Jen had been texting each other to confirm what the occupants in each car had already talked about amongst themselves—the long drives were starting to take their toll and each day they wanted rest breaks at shorter intervals.

'It feels good to stretch my legs,' Jen said. 'I wish we didn't have two hours to go.'

'We don't have a lot of choices,' Robert said. 'It's the next main town on the highway, and I don't think we should be stopping at any overnight rest areas where we'll probably be the only people.'

'Totally agree, given that we've seen that arsehole in two places now,' Craig said.

Jen didn't say anything, instead making her way back to the car.

Andie turned to Craig. 'What did you say that for?'

'What? It's not like Jen doesn't know that.'

'Yes, but she doesn't need to be reminded of it.'

'Let's make this a short break, then get back in the cars and keep moving,' Robert said.

As they were about to leave, another car pulled in. The driver didn't get out, but he didn't need to for them to see who it was.

'Everyone in the cars now,' Robert said. 'And lock the doors.'

Less than a minute later, they were back on the highway. For the next two hours, they checked if the car was still following them. And it was.

Andie texted Jen. *As soon as we get into town, we're going straight to the police station.*

Ok

Andie spent the rest of the drive wishing they were there already. Jen hadn't replied to her last text asking how she was feeling. When the Welcome to Port Headland sign came into view, Andie breathed a sigh of relief. Luckily, the police station was easy to find, and soon both cars were pulled up outside.

'I don't think we should all go in,' Robert said. 'Someone needs to watch the cars. I don't trust him, even if we are outside a police station.'

'We'll stay,' Andie said. 'You should go in with Jen.'

Andie and Craig waited outside and kept their eyes on the cars and the surrounding area. There was no sign of Eric.

'Surely he wouldn't be stupid enough to come up to us here,' Andie said.

Craig shook his head. 'I don't know about that. I think he's more out of control than we realise.'

Andie shivered. 'Let's hope the police can do something.'

But they couldn't. Half an hour later, when Jen and Robert came back out, Jen looked more scared than she did going in, and Robert was shaking his head and cursing under his breath.

'What's wrong?' Craig asked.

Robert stopped cursing long enough to answer. 'They can't do anything.'

'What do you mean they can't do anything,' Craig said.

'That's what they said.'

'But he's dangerous,' Andie said.

Robert nodded. 'We know that. But as far as the police are concerned, while his behaviour is odd, he actually hasn't done anything to any of us.'

Craig shook his head in disbelief. 'So, we're supposed to wait until he does something to one of us.'

Jen put her hands up. 'Stop. It won't be one of us. It will be me.'

Robert put his arm around her. 'We won't let anything happen to you.'

Craig nodded in agreement. 'If he tries to come anywhere near you, we'll stop him.'

Andie looked from Craig to Robert. They both had very determined looks on their faces. Would they be enough though?

'I think we should stay in a motel tonight that has better security than our caravans,' Robert said.

'Good idea,' Craig said. 'Let's find the one closest to the police station, just in case.'

They opted for Chinese that night. The restaurant was close to the motel they'd checked into, and Jen wasn't up for anything fancier. She hadn't wanted to go out at all, but there were no cooking facilities in their rooms. After an hour, they went back and had an early night, double-checking the locks on the room doors before turning in.

Even Jen slept well, feeling secure with the locked doors and screens on the windows. She woke feeling better than she had in the past few days, which didn't last long when she looked out the window.

'He's damaged our caravan.'

Robert jumped out of bed and looked out. Down below, the windows on their caravan had been smashed. He quickly threw on some clothes and opened the door to their room.

'Take Craig with you just in case he's still around.'

Robert banged on the door to Craig and Andie's room, and within a few minutes, Robert and Craig were in the car park looking at the caravan. Nothing appeared to have been stolen.

'We're calling the police,' Robert said.

Craig nodded. 'Now he's done something. The police should be able to help.'

When they arrived at the police station, they spoke with the same policeman Robert and Jen had spoken with the day before. When Robert showed him the photos of their caravan, the policeman said he'd come down straight away and take a look.

When he arrived, he took photos, spoke with Jen and said he'd follow up.

'At least that's something,' Andie said.

'Yes, but what does follow-up mean?' Craig said. 'We want him to scare that arsehole away so he doesn't come near Jen again.'

'I'm sure he'll do whatever he can within the law.'

'As long as that works.'

'What else can he do?'

'I don't know, but if it doesn't work, we'll have to do something.'

'What do you mean, we'll have to do something? Don't start thinking about doing anything stupid.'

'I wouldn't do that.'

Andie watched him as he turned away. She wasn't so sure about that.

The next day, Robert had a call from the police. They'd looked for Eric in town and couldn't locate him. But they would keep looking until they did.

'I guess we should stay then,' Robert said.

'Why?' Jen said. 'I want to be as far away from here as possible.'

Robert shook his head. 'I know you do, but we've finally got the police involved, and we need to stay until they sort something out. If we leave, Eric will just follow us again, and who knows how far we'd have to drive until we come across another police station. And besides, the caravan needs to be fixed.'

Jen didn't look happy, but she knew Robert was right.

'I think we should take turns standing guard tonight,' Craig said.

Andie turned to look at him. 'Do you think that's necessary?'

Craig nodded. 'We didn't do that last night, and look what happened.'

That night, Craig and Robert took turns staying awake. Andie offered to do a shift, but Craig was adamant that she stay inside with the door locked. She lay awake until Craig came back from his turn on watch. She tried to fall asleep, but the thoughts racing through her mind wouldn't let her. She was thinking of the first time they'd seen Eric in Kununurra and how far they'd travelled since then. The distance hadn't stopped him.

Suddenly there was a loud knock at the door, and she heard Robert call for Craig. He jumped out of bed and was outside before Andie knew what was happening. She followed and saw Craig and Robert confronting Eric in the car park. She picked up her phone and called 000, explaining the situation as quickly as possible. After she hung up, she kept repeating in her head, 'keep him there, keep him there...the police are on their way'.

Finally, she heard the siren. So did Eric. He turned to run, but Craig grabbed him first and tackled him to the ground. Robert wasn't far behind, and they kept him pinned to the ground until the police car pulled into the motel car park. Andie watched until she saw the police had handcuffed Eric before knocking on Jen's door.

'The police have got him.'

Jen walked out of the room, looked at the scene below and started crying. When she eventually stopped, she spoke.

'I want to leave first thing in the morning.'

Andie nodded. 'None of us will disagree with that.'

Four hours later, they were back on the road. Even though no one had much sleep, they didn't feel tired. Not even the long stretch of highway bothered them. The further away from Port Headland they got, the happier they all were. From the car, Andie sent Jen a text. *At least we're heading somewhere nice now.*

Jen didn't reply. Andie couldn't even imagine how Jen must feel but hoped the visit to Monkey Mia would cheer her up. Andie was looking forward to the white sandy beach and the wild dolphins that inhabited the waters. Such graceful creatures. Spending time watching them would be good for Andie's soul as well.

Chapter Eleven

It was a long way off the highway to get to Monkey Mia but when they arrived, watching the dolphins arc in and out of the cobalt water, the sun shining down on its surface and making it shimmer, was enough for them to forget the events of the past few days. Even Jen was mesmerized for a while by what she saw. By the time they'd arrived, it was late in the day, and even though Eric was no longer an issue, Jen still wanted to leave early the next morning and drive all the way to Perth, about 865 kilometres away. Andie would have liked to stay, but she couldn't ask that of Jen. In all the years they'd been friends, Jen had always been there for her. So, the next day they left at 4 am. Everyone was tired, but no one said anything. For Jen's sake, they were all happy to get on the road. That feeling changed after the first few hours as the highway dragged on, but they kept going and eventually reached the outskirts of Perth. That night was the earliest they'd gone to bed since setting out on their road trip, and the next morning no one wanted to get back in their cars. Regardless of hurrying the journey to Perth, they still arrived at the time they had planned on their itinerary, late July.

Before they started the exploration for the day, Andie updated the blog.

Monkey Mia

Seeing the dolphins in their natural habitat was a wonderful experience. And there were so many of them!

Seeing them did Jen a world of good, but Andie didn't add that detail. Jen had been smiling, and it was nice to see her take photos like she usually would.

The beautiful beach, and the rusty, red-coloured sand dunes, were also a highlight. We were lucky, as often, Monkey Mia can be busy, but yesterday, there was only one other group of people.

After watching the dolphins, we walked over the dunes and along the beach. And we also saw dugongs and turtles. The natural beauty, along with the peace and quiet, was just what we needed after the past few days.

Andie didn't add anything about the past few days. No one else needed to know what had happened.

No one was keen to sit on public transport after so many hours in the car, but they didn't want to miss the city. They caught a bus to Kings Park, the largest inner-city park in the world at 400 hectares, and lost track of time. By the time they walked through the different areas of the park, including the Western Australian Botanic Gardens, it was early afternoon. And Jen had taken a lot of photos, which Andie took as a good sign. Robert wanted to go somewhere nice for lunch, but Jen overruled him. They grabbed a sandwich and kept exploring the city instead.

Perth

What a beautiful city. After walking through Kings Park and taking in the amazing views of the city and its surrounds, we headed into the CBD. Jen found some shops she liked and bought a couple of things!

No one minded that Jen had wanted to look in the shops or that they had to wait while she tried things on. And Robert carried the shopping bags for her for the rest of the day.

Later in the day, we headed to Cottesloe Beach and watched the surfers in the clear aqua water, the waves coming in perfect arcs.

At sunset, we took a cruise along the Swan River, taking in the city skyline and the sights along the river, including the restored Swan Brewery. We all enjoyed the cruise and wished it had gone for longer.

Andie had particularly enjoyed the cruise, something about being on the water again touched her soul.

By the time they returned to the caravan park, talk had turned to what they'd do the following day. The discussion hadn't been going long before Robert convinced them to go on a winery tour in the Swan Valley. Craig thought the tour would be a waste of money, which Andie was pleased to hear him say. But

Robert was persuasive, so they found themselves leaving early the following morning on a minibus heading south. Their tour included four wineries and lunch, and by the end of the second winery, Andie hoped that Robert would slow down. He was trying everything there was on offer to taste, and he'd already bought three cartons. She heard Jen tell him to slow down, but he ignored her. He promised to behave himself at lunch at her request, but the minute Jen got up to go to the toilet, Robert ordered a bottle of wine to go with their food. The look on Jen's face when she came back said everything there was to say.

His behaviour only got worse at the third winery, and by the time they got to the fourth, even Andie was hoping the day would soon be over. No one at any of the wineries said anything though, probably because Robert was spending a lot of money. On the way back in the bus, he fell asleep. And Andie didn't write anything about that day in the blog.

The next morning, Robert pretended he wasn't hungover, but they all knew he was. And when they boarded the boat to take them to Rottnest Island for the day, he looked green, a look that only got worse the further out they went as the swell picked up. When they docked, he was the first one off and headed straight for the toilet. He didn't say anything when he came back, but he didn't need to. Craig was about to tease him, but Andie saw the look on Jen's face and whispered to Craig not to say anything. As the day progressed, Robert started to pick up. Jen mostly ignored him, which wasn't hard to do because we were all distracted by the quokkas, including Jen, who must have taken twenty photos.

'But they're beautiful,' she said when questioned about why she needed so many.

By the time they got back to the wharf in Fremantle, Robert seemed like himself again and suggested they all go out to dinner. He felt like Italian, he said, if that was all right with everyone. Andie and Craig nodded. Jen didn't say anything, and Andie wondered why. Yes, Robert's behaviour the day before hadn't been good, but Jen usually moved on from things quickly. Andie was surprised when they got to dinner and Robert ordered a bottle of wine. Surely, he'd had enough the day before.

The next day they went back to Fremantle, and even Craig noticed that Robert had picked a place for lunch that was licensed. The others were happy just to have a sandwich, but Robert kept insisting until they gave in. In the afternoon, they went down to the beach. They were heading east the next day, meaning it would be a while before they saw the ocean again. Surprisingly, the water was warm, and Andie wanted one more swim. As she bobbed and ducked through the waves, she thought about seeing if she could talk Craig into moving near a beach. But then she stopped herself. What she really wanted was to move to the coast by herself.

Chapter Twelve

This is the most desolate place I've ever seen, Andie thought to herself. No matter where she looked, there was nothing but desert and the occasional tree. No towns, no houses, not even a petrol station. Thankfully they'd filled up in Norseman before starting the 1200-kilometre trek across the Nullarbor Plain, eventually arriving in Ceduna in South Australia. There would be some towns along the way, but they hadn't seen one yet. And although the trek had just started, Andie wished it was over. She still hadn't told Craig about the decision she'd finally made while swimming in the ocean in Fremantle. It was all she'd been thinking about since. No one seemed to notice, or mention, that she hadn't written a blog entry about Fremantle or Rottnest Island.

She knew she would have to tell him, but what did that mean for the rest of the trip? They still had a long way to go to get to South Australia. Then there was Tasmania. Then they had to head up through Victoria and New South Wales before crossing the border into their home state. If she told him now, they'd have to end the trip, and Craig was having such a good time. She didn't want to ruin that. She felt she owed him at least that after all the years they'd spent together. She just didn't know if she could fake how she felt for the rest of the trip.

They'd planned for the trip across the Nullarbor to take six days. Apparently, there was a lot to see, even though that wasn't the impression Andie had so far. The first day's journey took them as far as Kalgoorlie, and while there, they visited the tourist mine. Even Robert was intrigued by what they saw. Although, Andie suspected it was because of the technical aspects of how the mine used to operate that the tour guide went through in detail. Along with how much money it had been worth.

Andie was also fascinated as they went underground. She'd never gone this far down before, and she'd been worried that she'd feel claustrophobic. But being underground didn't bother her at all. For Jen, though, it was a different story. They'd only been down there five minutes when she could hear Jen's breathing become shallow.

'I don't like this. I'm going back up to the surface.'

Robert turned to look at her. 'But this is interesting.'

Jen shook her head. 'I don't care. I don't want to be here.'

'But you'll probably never get a chance to do this again.'

'It's horrible. I feel trapped like at any moment the walls will cave in, and we'll be buried alive.'

'Now you are being silly. We're not going to be buried alive. There wouldn't be any tours down here if it weren't safe.'

'How do you know? Who knows when they last checked the safety of this mine.'

'I'm sure they do it all the time.'

'Maybe they don't. Anyway, it doesn't matter. I'm leaving.'

Andie watched as Jen went back to the lift that went up the mine shaft.

'She'll regret it,' Robert said.

'I can't believe how irrational you were behaving down there,' Robert said to Jen when they were back at the caravan park.

'I wasn't being irrational. I was scared. I felt like I couldn't breathe.'

'There was no reason to feel scared. I told you it was perfectly safe.'

'And how would you know? Are you a mining safety engineer?'

'I don't need to be one of those to know we would be fine down there.'

'Well, I didn't feel that way.'

'Well, you should have.'

'Don't tell me how I should feel.'

'I'm not telling you how you should feel. I just think you were wrong.'

'It can't be wrong if it's how I feel.'

'Well, it was.'

'So, you are telling me how I should feel?'

'No, I said I wasn't.'

'Sounds like you are.'

'I don't want to talk about this anymore. It's ridiculous.'

'Oh, like me when I was underground.'

'I didn't mean that.'

'I think you did.'

'Enough of this.'

'Don't walk away.'

But Robert didn't listen and went inside the caravan, shutting the door behind him. Jen turned and walked towards the tables in the BBQ area. From where Andie was, she could see that Jen was crying. She debated whether or not to go over but decided to give her a few minutes on her own first. It looked like she could use it. Andie couldn't understand why Robert had reacted the way he had. Jen had clearly been scared when they were underground. She couldn't remember Jen mentioning being claustrophobic, but something had happened.

'Are you all right?' Andie asked, sitting down beside Jen five minutes later.

'I am now. I don't know why I felt trapped down there. It just came upon me all of a sudden.'

'And Robert didn't help?'

Jen nodded. 'I wish he wouldn't be so unwilling to look at things from other people's perspectives.'

'Maybe he'll realise that his reaction didn't help.'

Jen shook her head. 'As far as he's concerned, the subject is closed. Can we talk about something else? What's the plan for tomorrow?'

'Didn't Robert want to drive to Border Village?'

'Yes. He doesn't think it's worth stopping anywhere on the way.'

'Did he check?

'I don't think so. You know what he's like. He just wants to get to the next city.'

'We'll have a look then. And we better do it before we leave Kalgoorlie because I doubt we'll have internet for the next few days.'

'Ok.'

'Are you ready to head back?'

'I guess so. I can't stay here for the rest of the day.'

As they walked back, Andie had the impression that even though Jen said that, she would have been happy to stay there for the rest of the day, away from Robert.

Only a few days ago, Jen had felt all the original feelings she'd had for Robert and for the first time in a long time, she felt confident that things would be okay. Now, she wasn't so sure. Now she was feeling confused all over again.

Kalgoorlie

As well as seeing the tourist mine, we also visited the Super Pit. At 3.5 kilometres long, 1.5 kilometres wide and more than 600 metres deep, you can see it from space. None of us had ever seen anything like it.

Which is why Robert probably agreed to go, Andie thought to herself. After he'd heard all the information about the running and the profits at the tourist mine, he'd gone back to losing interest in mining again.

We didn't do the tour, but we did go to the lookout, which gave us a great vantage point to take in its size. For many

years, it was Australia's largest open-cut gold mine. Gold
mining has been a major industry in Kalgoorlie since 1893, and
many of the buildings reflect the grandeur of the gold rush era.

By the time they headed off the next day, they'd convinced Robert to stay at one more town on the Nullarbor. All it took was a mention of Australia's longest, straight stretch of road to get him to agree. At 147 kilometres long and with nothing to see, he'd be bored before they even got halfway. So, they were stopping for the night in Madura.

Later that morning, as Andie sat in the passenger seat, she wondered how she would cope with the rest of the drive across the Nullarbor. There would be nothing to keep her mind distracted. Or provide her with topics of conversation so that she doesn't blurt out anything about her decision.

'Isn't this great,' Craig said, interrupting her thoughts. 'Look where we are. This is one of the greatest adventure drives anywhere in the world.'

'I'm not sure how much adventure there will be when there's nothing out here.'

'That's the point. It's you against the elements, and if something happens out here, you're on your own.'

'Then let's hope nothing happens.'

As he spoke, she looked at him. If only she'd been sure before they left home. She wouldn't be in the mess she was in now.

That afternoon, they pulled into the Madura roadhouse. As they got out of the cars, they saw sheep grazing on the grounds. It was an odd sight but a welcome one after the empty lands that had defined the day's drive.

'Tomorrow's stop is Border Village,' Robert said after they'd set up for the night.

Jen turned to look at him. 'You can't wait to finish this part of the trip, can you?'

Robert nodded. 'Absolutely. There's just nothing here.'

'But that's why it's great,' Craig said. 'It's so different to where we've been so far, and we won't see anything else like it for the rest of the trip.'

Robert looked around him. 'Thank goodness for that. Now, I'm going to ask the staff in the roadhouse if they'd like to join us for a drink. Have we got any of that cheese left from last night?'

Jen nodded, although she didn't look happy, which Andie suspected was more about the drinking than the cheese.

'Great. Let's do up a platter. I'll go over to the roadhouse.'

Craig turned to look in the direction of the building. 'I think they'll be working for a few more hours yet.'

Robert shrugged. 'They can see any customers who come in from here. I don't imagine they're expecting an influx. I haven't seen anyone else arrive since we pulled up.'

Andie watched as he walked towards the door. 'Is that his way of saying he's over our company?'

Jen shook her head. 'No, I think he's over my company, not yours.'

'Is he still annoyed about Kalgoorlie?' Andie said.

'Who knows? Anyway, it would be interesting to hear what it's like living out here.'

Andie nodded in agreement. 'And I think we're about to find out if we get to hear that information.'

Jen turned to see Robert walking back towards them.

'That didn't take long,' she said when he returned.

'I only had to mention joining us for a drink, and the manager was in. He's glad about the company. The others need to head off. They've got a long drive in front of them.'

While they waited for the manager to join them, Andie took the opportunity to update the blog. She'd have to wait until they got closer to Adelaide before having the internet connection she needed to post, but at least she could get the information ready.

Nullarbor

We headed off on the Eyre Highway, ready to begin our Nullarbor Plain crossing. The name Nullarbor is from the Latin, meaning no trees, although we did see some scrub. And it covers around 200,000 square kilometres. Most of which we definitely won't be seeing! Even though we have 4WDs, the caravans aren't made for the off-roading you need to do out here.

The towns we've been through so far include Norseman, Kalgoorlie, Balladonia, and Caiguna. And we've still got a way to go! Even though it's a mostly barren landscape and often forbidding, we did see some wild camels and kangaroos. Very few people, though.

It's also very cold. Even though it's August and therefore, winter, it's still colder than we expected it to be. I'm glad I packed an extra blanket!

We've stopped for tonight at the Madura Roadhouse and will soon be having drinks with the manager. We're all looking forward to hearing what it's like living out here.

Half an hour later, Marty, the roadhouse manager, joined them. Robert and Craig were already onto their second drink. Andie and Jen were taking things slowly.

'It must take a special person to live out here,' Andie said.

Marty nodded. 'You have to like the isolation. I grew up on a property about 100 kilometres from the nearest town, so I'm used to it.'

'You didn't want to stay on the property?' Craig asked.

Marty nodded. 'I did, but the drought killed us. Had to sell the place.'

'I'm sorry to hear that,' Jen said.

'Yeah, Mum and Dad took it hard. They'd lived there and worked the property for thirty-five years.'

'Where did they go?' Robert asked.

'They moved right away. They didn't want to move into the town where everyone knew them, so they went over the border and bought a small place at Glenelg. They wanted the opposite of the outback, so they chose the beach. Luckily there was enough money from the sale of the property to get a small house.'

'That would have been so hard for them,' Jen said.

Marty nodded again. 'Especially as there was no money left after they bought the house, they both had to get jobs. Which wasn't easy as the only thing they knew was working the land.'

'You've never thought about moving closer to them?' Andie asked.

He shook his head. 'I like it out here. The beach where they are is nice, but there are too many people around. My parents didn't like that at first, although they're used to it now.'

'Do you see them often?' Jen asked.

'A couple of times a year. As much as I don't like crowds, I need to get supplies, and there are some things you can only get in the city, so I stop in Adelaide before I head back.'

'What do you do if you run out of something?' Craig asked.

'Either do without or contact one of the truckies I know and hope they're coming this way. If they are, they'll pick up whatever I need and drop it off when they stop to refuel or to have a rest.'

'That's good of them,' Robert said.

'It's common here and in other remote places around the country. It would be hard without them.'

'Are you married?' Andie asked.

Marty shook his head. 'I was engaged once, but she didn't like it here. Too remote for her.'

'That's a shame,' Craig said. 'Guessing it's not easy to meet someone out here.'

Marty shook his head again. 'No, it's not. That's why I thought I was lucky, but after six months, she changed her mind. That's how long it took for the novelty of the place to wear off.'

Andie looked at Craig. Should she change her mind? Marty looked sad as he spoke about his ex-fiancé. Was it better to be with someone, even if you knew it was no longer right, than be on your own?

That thought was still with Andie as they all turned in for the night. She didn't fall asleep though. Craig had drunk too much beer and was snoring. Andie looked out the window and saw the light on in the roadhouse and Marty sitting out the back with a beer in his hand. She was surprised he was still drinking until she remembered that he'd only had three beers while they were talking, unlike Craig. And unlike Robert with his wine. She decided to get out of bed and see if he wanted some company.

'Hi, Marty. Do you mind if I join you?'

Marty shook his head.

'I can't sleep, and there isn't much to do around here.'

Marty laughed. 'So, you came over because there is nothing else to do.'

Andie laughed. 'I didn't mean it that way.'

Marty smiled. 'I know. Would you like a beer?'

Andie shook her head. 'I'm not a big fan of beer.'

'I think I've got a bottle of wine inside.'

'That would be nice.'

Andie watched as he went inside to find the wine. She couldn't help but notice how attractive he was, and she couldn't stop looking at him through the window. It had been a long time since she'd looked at Craig that way.

'Here you go. I hope it's all right. I don't drink wine. An older couple who stopped here gave it to me after I helped change their car tyre.'

The time passed quickly as they sat and talked, Andie drinking more wine than she intended. Marty didn't seem in any hurry for her to leave. In fact, he'd moved his chair closer at some point, probably when Andie had gone inside to use the bathroom. Their chairs were so close they were almost touching. Andie debated for a moment about moving her chair away, but she didn't. Instead, she took another sip of her wine and looked up at the stars.

'It's beautiful out here. You can't see the stars like this in the city.'

Marty nodded. 'That's not the only thing that's beautiful out here.'

Andie was glad it was dark. She could feel herself blushing and thinking she could say the same thing about him. Instead, she asked if he ever got lonely.

Marty nodded. 'All the time. The others that work here provide some company, but it's not the same as being close to someone.'

'Are the others here all the time?'

Marty shook his head. 'They come for a few days to help out, then go back to their families. I'm the only one who's here all the time.'

'It's a shame your fiancé left.'

'Yes, I thought we were going be together for the rest of our lives, but it didn't turn out that way.'

'Have you tried looking for someone else?'

Marty nodded. 'Yes, but who's coming out here? I will be on my own, or I'll have to move. I don't like either option.'

'You're not on your own tonight.'

'I know. But you're married.'

'I know that.'

Andie looked at him for a few moments trying to decide what to do. She knew what she wanted to do, but she also knew that it was the wrong thing to do. No matter how she felt about her marriage and Craig, she couldn't do that to him. She finished her wine and stood up.

'I should probably go back to my caravan.'

'Yes, you probably should.'

Andie looked at him for a few more moments before slowly turning around, walking back to the caravan and getting into bed beside Craig. It took her a long time to fall asleep.

'Everyone ready to go?' Robert said the next morning.

Andie nodded. The sooner they left, the better.

'I've checked the map, and it's not much further to go from Border Village to Ceduna, so we may as well continue on.'

Andie smiled to herself. Robert was determined to get them to Adelaide and away from the outback. 'Are we stopping anywhere on the way?'

Robert nodded. 'We'll stop at the Great Australian Bight. It's next to the highway.'

Andie smiled again. Trust Robert to pick the one thing they didn't have to detour off the highway to see. But she was glad they were stopping. She was interested and knew Jen was already thinking about the photos she'd take. And she was glad that Jen had whispered to her that Robert had apologised for his behaviour in Kalgoorlie.

'What about after that?' Craig asked.

'More typical Nullarbor country,' Robert said. 'Endless plains with no trees. We can stop at the Nullarbor Roadhouse and get petrol. From the roadhouse, it's another two hundred and ninety-six kilometres to Ceduna.'

Great Australian Bight

We were speechless when we stopped at the Great Australian Bight, with its sheer cliffs dropping straight into the ocean. The wildness of it was something we'd never experienced before. As Jen took photo after photo and Craig and Robert walked along the path, I stood still, feeling the wind rush against me, eyes fixed on the dark blue, choppy ocean. Right in front of me, I saw a whale breach the water before disappearing again. After pointing it out to the others, I thought about the whale, free to swim where it wanted.

She was still thinking about the whale as she wrote the blog entry later when they'd set up in Ceduna for the night. Robert looked happy that they were closer to Adelaide. Until he looked at the map and realised there were still 600 kilometres to go. As much as he wanted to get there, he didn't want to drive that far in a day, so he reluctantly agreed to spend the following night in Whyalla.

'At least Whyalla is on the coast, so we'll have the ocean to look at,' Robert said, not realising that it was a port city rather than a seaside resort.

Craig looked around him after they arrived. 'Glad we're just staying here one night. It looks like there's a red haze to everything.'

Jen looked up from her phone. 'According to this website, sometimes there's powdery iron ore that gets blown over the city from the steelworks.'

'That can't be good for you,' Craig said.

'There's a lookout we could go to,' Jen said. 'It has 360-degree views across the city, the Spencer Gulf, and down the coast.'

Andie would have been content to do nothing that afternoon. There were too many thoughts rushing through her mind to be able to take anything else in. But she went anyway.

She stayed away from the others, pretending she was intently interested in the view. She was glad the others decided to have an early night so they could head off first thing in the morning.

The highway was busier than any other point across the Nullarbor, and Andie didn't like it. It was the road trains that unsettled her, flying by at well over the one-hundred-kilometre an hour limit, the trailers at the back swaying across the road. So far, two of them had been closer than Andie would have liked. But neither of those got as close as the one that didn't leave enough room when it pulled back into the left lane in front of Jen and Robert—causing Robert to swerve off the highway and across the barren landscape beside them.

'Bloody hell,' Robert said as he stood beside the car. 'What did that idiot think he was doing? He could have killed us.'

'I don't think he cared,' Craig said. 'He just wants to get to his destination as fast as possible.'

'Are you all right, Jen?' Andie said.

Jen nodded her head. 'I'll be fine. Just a bit shaken up.'

Andie looked at her. She'd already had enough drama for this trip.

Robert came over and put his arm around her. 'Are you sure you're all right?'

Jen nodded again. 'What about you? It was your side of the car he almost hit.'

'I'm fine. I can't believe how close he was. I felt like I could reach out the window and touch the last trailer.'

From where she was standing, Andie could see the looks of concern on both their faces. And how much it meant to each of them that the other was all right.

'Luckily, you didn't have to swerve too much,' Craig said. 'Otherwise, the caravan might have turned over.'

Andie glared at him. Couldn't he see they were both shaken? Why did he have to bring that up?

As she and Jen waited while the men went over the car and caravan, Andie wished they'd hurry up. She'd had enough of the outback now. And of Craig.

Chapter Thirteen

The first thing Robert did when they arrived in Adelaide was reserve a table at a fancy restaurant. Craig had never been a fan of fine dining, but even he kept his mouth shut after the experience that Robert and Jen had with the road train. And Andie didn't think about the budget once. They'd hardly spent anything over the past few days. And there was something soothing about the crisp white tablecloths, dim lighting and unobtrusive waitstaff who seemed to glide across the floor, appearing when anyone turned to look for one.

'What's the plan for tomorrow?' Andie asked while they waited for the meals to be brought out. 'There's a lot to see while we're here. I'd like to go to the Adelaide Central Markets.'

Jen nodded. 'I've heard of them as well. We could buy lots of nice cheeses and olives.'

'I want to go to the Adelaide Oval,' Craig said. 'There's a tour you can do that looks interesting.'

'And we also have to go to the Adelaide Hills to Hahndorf,' Jen said.

'We need to visit Glenelg as well,' Andie added, trying not to think about Marty.

'You've all forgotten the most important place to visit,' Robert said. 'The wine regions. I've done some research and found two tours – one to McLaren Vale and one to the Barossa.'

'Do we need to do both?' Craig said.

Robert nodded. 'Absolutely. We can't come all this way and not see both.'

Andie knew Craig wouldn't be interested in another wine tour, but she didn't say anything. She was too busy hoping Robert didn't drink as much as he did on the last one.

'Sounds like we're going to have a full itinerary while we're here,' Jen said.

Robert nodded. 'A toast then. To seeing everything we can fit in.'

Jen watched the others at the table as they ate and drank. The near miss had scared her more than she wanted to admit. It also made her re-evaluate her feelings for Robert. Again.

The next morning, they boarded the bus for the first of the wine tours Robert had booked the night before. He'd found one that started with a half-day tour of McLaren Vale, then went on to Glenelg in the afternoon, with an option to stay longer and catch the tram back to the city. Not long after she'd taken her seat, Andie was pleased to realise that the other people on the tour seemed lovely. There was a couple from Spain, as well as couples from Hobart and Sydney. But for the first part of the trip, she sat silently, not joining in any conversations, instead preferring to gaze out the window at the passing countryside. She'd been awake half the night thinking about Craig. She was finding it extremely hard to push her feelings down anymore. Spending the rest of her life with him wasn't what she wanted to do. The thought of starting over scared her, but not as much as being unhappy for the rest of her life. She just wished she wasn't having these thoughts on a wine tour. She'd have to watch what she drank so she didn't blurt something out. The only thing left was to decide when to tell him.

'Here we are at our first stop,' their driver said. 'After you get off the bus, walk straight ahead under the archway and then turn left. You'll see a long table set up under the trees.'

Andie looked around them as they walked to the table. All the other couples were holding hands. Except for her and Craig. And Jen and Robert. This surprised Andie as they seemed to be getting along well lately, especially after the near miss. She sat at the table and looked at the view—rolling hills, vines, clear blue skies and a scattering of large, shady trees like the ones they were sitting under. The first of the wines was poured, and Andie took a small sip and then tipped the rest out. No matter what, she had to keep her mind straight today.

'If you don't like it, I'll finish it for you,' Robert said.

'No, I'll do that,' Craig said.

Andie turned to look at him. 'You don't usually like wine tastings.'

'That's not the point. I might like something I try here.'

Whatever, Andie thought to herself. She didn't want to give either of them the wine. They'd consume enough during the day, and she didn't want to add to their total.

Beside her, the couple from Sydney were asking Jen about their trip.

'What a wonderful thing to do,' the woman said.

Her husband nodded. 'We've talked about it before but haven't taken the plunge and headed off. I assume you'll be stopping in Sydney?'

Jen nodded.

'Have you been before?' he said.

'I'm there a lot for work, but I never have time to do anything but go from the airport to the office and back again.'

'We'll have to give you some tips on things to do that aren't on the usual tourist lists,' she said.

So, while they progressed through their first tastings of the day, Jen added notes to her phone about places and restaurants they recommended. The longer they talked, the more excited Jen became. She was looking forward to being able to see something other than the inside of the office. Surprisingly,

Robert didn't join in the conversation. Considering how he'd been about their itinerary, Andie wondered why. But every time she looked over at him, he was talking to the winery staff who were pouring the tastings and convincing them that if there was only a drop left in the bottle, he might as well finish it. Andie didn't know how he was doing it. It was only 11 am.

By the time they'd finished the tasting, Jen had already talked to the couple from Hobart and had tips from them. Andie didn't hear what they said. She was in the middle of a conversation with the Spanish couple.

'We've been here three weeks now, and we still can't believe the distances between places and how big your country is,' he said. 'You must spend a lot of time driving on your trip.'

Andie nodded. 'We do.'

'If we drove as far as you need to between some of your towns, we'd be several countries away,' she said.

'That must be nice though. You can visit a lot of places easily. Everywhere for us is a long way.'

'Yes, we make a lot of short trips to other countries,' she said. 'This is the furthest away from home we've ever been.'

Andie wanted to know more about the short trips they'd taken and spent the next few minutes finding out about the places they'd been. The more she listened, the more she wanted to visit those places. After the trip she was on was over, there wouldn't be any reason not to go once she'd saved the money. She'd only need to save enough for herself.

Andie continued to talk to the Spanish couple until they boarded the bus for the drive to the next winery. She hadn't spoken to Craig at all. For some reason, he'd been attentive to what Robert and the winery staff were saying. On the way to the next winery, he regaled her with what he'd learnt about the wines they'd tasted. Andie would have rather looked at the scenery out the window, but Craig seemed so pleased by his new-found knowledge that she listened. She didn't want to raise any suspicions. Not that he would have noticed anyway.

At the next winery, Andie didn't like any of the wines they tasted. From the look on Robert's face, he didn't seem to be enjoying them either. But he still drank everything they put in front of him. By the time they got to the fourth winery, he was unsteady on his feet. But he kept being given tastings, and no one said anything. She could see Jen was keeping an eye on him. At the last winery, whenever he turned his back, Jen poured out the wine he'd been given. Robert didn't seem to notice.

Jen looked relieved when they got off the bus in Glenelg. No more wineries for the day. That was until Robert saw a bar set up on the beach.

'That looks good. Let's go.'

Andie watched as Robert headed towards the entrance and then somehow walked in without the bouncers stopping him, even though he wasn't walking in a straight line. He went to the front row of deck chairs lined up on the sand and pulled four of them together.

'Didn't they have a reserved sign on them?' Jen asked.

Robert shrugged. 'Not anymore.'

Andie looked around, but no one seemed to notice that Robert had moved the reserved sign to the row of chairs behind them.

'Right,' Robert said. 'What are we having to drink?'

Craig turned to look at the bar. 'I'll have a beer.'

Robert nodded. 'Good idea. What about the ladies?'

Jen put her hand on Robert's shoulder. 'I think you've had enough.'

Robert shook his head. 'Not even close to having enough. I'll get Craig and me a beer while you two make up your mind about what you want.'

Andie saw the look on Jen's face as Robert walked to the bar. 'I don't need any more to drink.'

'Me either,' Jen said. 'If I could only get Robert to think like that.'

'He likes a drink, doesn't he?'

'That's one way of putting it.'

Before long, he was back, and the guys sat down on the deck chairs with their beers and looked out at the ocean.

'I might go for a walk,' Jen said.

'I'll come with you if you like,' Andie said.

Jen shook her head. 'No, stay here and enjoy the view. I won't be long.'

Andie watched her as she left but didn't try and follow her. Beside her, Craig and Robert were talking, and neither seemed to remember she was still there. She could only hope they'd be happy to leave soon and go back to the caravan park. The thought of a long, hot shower was extremely appealing, but she didn't want to leave the guys drinking down by the beach. She didn't trust them to get on the tram back to the city by themselves.

Thankfully it was Craig who mentioned being hungry, which gave Andie a chance to say there was a good restaurant near the caravan park. They just needed to wait for Jen to get back.

Jen hadn't walked as far as she'd planned. Only around the corner before finding a seat. She had too much on her mind to take in the sights around her, so she decided she might as well stop.

Ever since the incident with Eric, she'd felt like she and Robert were heading in the direction she wanted. She'd felt happy most of the time. There had been occasions when Robert had driven her crazy. But she'd become more accepting of that. No one was perfect, and on the whole, things had been better between them. If only she could get him to cut down his alcohol consumption. She didn't like who he became when he drank.

On the way back on the tram, Robert and Craig fell asleep, and it was up to Andie and Jen to wake them when the time came. All thoughts of dinner together were forgotten as Andie and Jen put their husbands to bed. Jen wasn't hungry and said she wanted to go for another walk. So, Andie headed out to dinner by herself. She found a cheaper restaurant than the one she'd mentioned earlier, sat at the table in the back corner and ordered a plate of pasta. She shook her head when the waiter asked if she wanted to see the wine list. What would happen when they went on the second wine tour that Robert had organised?

As she waited for her food, she pulled her laptop out of her bag and began typing, even though she felt too preoccupied with her feelings towards Craig to focus on the blog.

McLaren Vale and Glenelg

We spent a lovely day in McLaren Vale, 40 kilometres south of Adelaide. The area is famous as a wine-growing region, with grapes first planted in the area around 1838. Today there are more than 88 cellar doors. We were pleased to hear that a lot of them were family-owned and run or small boutique wineries. Of course, we couldn't verify that ourselves as it would take a long time to visit them, and we only had half a day. But a couple of wineries we visited definitely fell into those categories. It was lovely when we got to talk to the staff during our visits and hear their passion for what they do.

As Andie typed that last sentence, a thought in the back of her mind came to the fore. A thought that she'd been ignoring for several weeks as she'd been too concerned with the state of her marriage. It was a thought that was linked to her future. About her job. She wasn't sure she wanted to go back to teaching. As much as she'd loved it, the things she'd seen on this trip, the experiences she'd had, and the possibility of moving from the city to a smaller, beachside town led her to rethink her career. Maybe it was time to try something new there as well. Or would that be too much?

McLaren Vale is known for its dry red wines, particularly Shiraz, as the climate around McLaren Vale works well with that variety.

Remembering that morning and Robert's behaviour, she decided that was enough information about wine for this blog entry.

Glenelg was a surprise for all of us. Such a beautiful seaside town close to Adelaide, just a tram ride away. We spent time at a beach club, sitting in deck chairs, gazing out over the ocean. Swimming would have been nice, but the water was too cold. Even if it wasn't, we didn't have our togs with us anyway.

The Art Deco buildings dotted through the suburb are worth seeing too.

Not that Andie had much of a chance to see any buildings other than the ones they could see near the beach and the tram line. Her train of thought was interrupted by the waiter bringing her dinner. It was good timing as her thoughts started turning towards Marty and how she'd felt that night.

Thankfully they had a break between wine tours, and the next morning they all got in Andie and Craig's car and drove an hour north to go on a Murray River cruise on a paddle wheeler. Robert had said he would drive, but Andie didn't trust the alcohol was out of his system. She didn't tell him that. Instead, she said that she'd had a good night's sleep and was wide awake, so would drive them.

Not long into the cruise, Andie was glad they'd booked it. She enjoyed standing on the deck with a breeze blowing, watching the countryside go by. Thirty minutes in, Andie noticed a small cabin near the riverbank. As they got closer, she could see a woman outside. There were no other cabins around. As the boat came in line with the cabin, Andie could see the woman clearly, and she looked older than Andie. There didn't seem to be anyone else around. Clothes were hanging on the line. Just women's clothes, enough for one person. How had she decided to live out here by herself? That is, if she was by herself. And if she was, was she happy? And could Andie be happy?

Murray River

The Murray River is the longest river in the country at 2,508 km. Obviously, we could only see a small portion of that. But what we did see was beautiful. And being on the paddle wheeler was fun. It reminded us of being in Longreach, which seems so long ago now. We can't believe how quickly this trip is going!

Not as quickly as Andie would have liked, she thought, as she typed at the end of the day.

The river was calm and flowing gracefully. The landscape was uniquely Australian, and the peace and quiet we experienced was a nice change of pace from the noises of the city.

She stopped typing. The fact that Jen and Robert weren't talking, and she and Craig hardly spoke, contributed to the peace and quiet. She didn't add that though.

The second wine tour Robert organised involved more driving and more chances to look at the passing scenery. Plus, this one only visited four wineries and included lunch at the oldest of the wineries they'd be visiting. Maybe with all the driving and the chance to walk around a small country town, there would be less time for drinking. Andie didn't feel like doing a wine tour at all, but Robert had been excited about it at breakfast. Even Craig was looking forward to it. On the way out there, Andie kept hoping they'd both behave themselves. She looked around the bus, and nobody else seemed like the type of people who would get carried away. This was definitely a different crowd from the last one. No one introduced themselves when they first got on the bus, and no one talked on the trip out. It was going to be an interesting day.

At the first winery, Robert tried everything and bought a few bottles to take with him. Craig tried everything too but didn't find anything he liked enough to buy. Everyone else in the group stood around and tried a few but didn't buy anything either. And none of them seemed interested in what they were being told about the wine or the winery.

By the third winery, Robert had bought twelve bottles and tried everything offered on the tastings. Thankfully the third winery was also the lunch stop.

'This looks like a nice place,' Robert said. 'Are we doing the tasting before lunch?'

The driver nodded. 'That way, you can buy a bottle you like to have with your lunch.'

'Good idea,' Robert said.

Andie and Jen looked at each other. Robert certainly didn't need a bottle with lunch. But unfortunately, he bought one anyway.

When the food came out, Andie and Jen both looked at it in dismay. The platter with cold meats, cheeses, bread, and dips looked delicious, but it wouldn't be enough to soak up the wine

Robert had drunk. As she looked at it, Andie wondered if they could order more bread. Not that it would do any good. Robert seemed more interested in drinking the wine than eating the food. No matter how many times Jen said he should eat his lunch. Craig wasn't being helpful either. He suggested they get another bottle, which Andie and Jen both said was a bad idea. Robert got up anyway and bought another one.

'Let's go and sit under the trees,' Robert said. 'I don't want any more food.'

Craig nodded. 'Good idea.'

Andie watched as Robert got up and headed outside. He was unsteady on his feet, but no one other than herself and Jen noticed. Everyone else at the table was still eating their lunch and talking. A few wines had made the quiet group from earlier this morning into a loud bunch. Jen found the closest tree with a table under it and got Robert to sit down.

'I think you've had enough. We've still got another winery and then an hour drive back to Adelaide.'

'Another winery. Great.'

'No, it's not great. You're drunk.'

'No, I'm not. I'm enjoying myself.'

Andie looked on as Robert picked up the new bottle and topped up his glass.

'What are you doing?' Jen said. 'Enough. You can't walk straight.'

'Yes, I can. Now leave me alone.'

Andie watched as Robert got up and went over to another table. Craig, being his usual helpful self, topped up his glass, walked over and sat down with Robert. While their backs were turned, Jen tipped out some wine from the bottle.

'He won't notice?' Andie said.

Jen shook her head. 'I wish we were going back now.'

'Maybe we can distract him at the next one.'

Jen nodded. 'Good idea. Let's get him talking to someone else so he doesn't notice the wine being poured.'

It turned out to be a good plan, and Robert only tried two wines at the last winery. On the bus, on the way back, he fell asleep. At least he wasn't talking rubbish anymore, and Jen only had to stop him snoring once.

'Wouldn't be the first time,' their driver said as they got off the bus, Jen holding on to Robert.

'I'm sure it's not, but by his age, he should know better,' Jen said.

For the second night in a row, Craig and Robert went to bed early, although Robert went first—as soon as they'd got back to the caravan. Looks like another dinner on my own,

Andie thought. But tonight, Jen decided to join her. She needed to talk.

'I've known for a while,' Jen said. 'I don't know what to do. He won't admit he has a problem.'

'How long has it been going on?'

'For about eighteen months before we left. It started because of the stress from work. I thought the trip would help.'

'Was he drinking every day?'

Jen nodded. 'Some days less than others, but yes, every day.'

'Did he go to bars?'

Jen shook her head. 'Not a lot. Only if he went after work with people from the office. He mostly drank at home. That way, no one else could see him if he had too much.'

'We've seen him now. Do you think that might help?'

Jen sighed. 'I'd like to think so, although he didn't think he had a problem even after the McLaren Vale trip. He thinks he just got carried away.'

'How many times have you had the conversation with him?'

'Too many to count.'

Andie reached over and squeezed Jen's hand. If Robert wouldn't admit he had a problem, then he wouldn't be interested in addressing it.

'Let's change the subject,' Jen said. 'I want to enjoy dinner and forget about today.'

So, they talked about the highlights of their trip so far. And Jen mentioned how much she enjoyed not working twelve hours a day.

'And I'm loving our blog.'

Andie smiled. Even though there were plenty of times she hadn't felt like writing in it, today being one of those days, she did enjoy it when she was in the right mood. She liked using her creative side. It was something she wanted to do more. Maybe when the trip was over, she would think about a different career. Something more creative. But for now, she wanted to forget the whole day, and she didn't think anyone would notice that she hadn't done an entry.

'I knew it,' Craig said the next morning as they prepared to head off.

Andie turned to look at him. 'You're not far behind. You've had a drink every day since we started this trip.'

'But I didn't at home. And besides, we're on holidays.'

'Stop using that excuse.'

'I haven't seen you have too many days without a drink.'

Andie thought about what Craig had said. He was right. She may not have been drinking anywhere near the level that Robert was, or even Craig, but it had been most days so far. She decided things would be different for the rest of the trip.

The next morning, Robert was quieter than usual but insistent that it was because he was tired, not because he was hungover. Jen said she would drive that day, and he didn't say anything. They had four and a half hours in front of them to reach that day's destination of Mt Gambier. One night there, and the following day they'd be heading over the border to Victoria.

The drive was uneventful, and Jen was relieved. She was still shaken by their near miss. Robert slept most of the way, which made her happy as he had no opportunity to say anything about her driving.

After arriving, they decided to look around Mt Gambier and then drive another twenty-five kilometres to Racecourse Bay and stay in a caravan park with a view of the harbour. They'd had enough of seeing the inland over the past few weeks and wanted to balance that out with a night by the water.

Mt Gambier

We ventured around town, taking in the sights, with our last stop being Blue Lake. We were all excited about seeing it, having seen pictures during our research of things to do in the area. But when we got there, we were disappointed. It turns out the lake is only the bright cobalt blue colour we'd seen in pictures between December and March each year. The rest of the year, it's the steel grey colour we saw today. We did some more research and found that there doesn't seem to be an agreed-upon reason for the change. The most popular theory is that it has something to do with the water temperature in the lake. So instead of spending more time looking at the lake, we headed off on the surrounding walking trails. Well, Jen and I did. Craig and Robert stayed behind.

When they'd got back, Robert was just waking up after falling asleep in the caravan. And he and Jen had exchanged words.

'You missed a beautiful walk,' Jen had said.

'I didn't feel like walking. We've done a lot of that lately.'

'The walk would have done you good, especially since you have a hangover.'

'I don't have a hangover. I've told you that already.'

'Don't lie. We all saw how much you drank yesterday.'

'I didn't drink that much.'

'You fell asleep on the bus on the way back.'

'I was tired.'

'No, you weren't. You were drunk. You drink too much.'

'No, I don't.'

'Yes, you do. And it's time you did something about it.'

'I don't want to listen to this anymore. I'm going for a walk.'

Jen had shaken her head. Now he wants to go for a walk, she thought to herself.

Andie had moved away, but she'd still heard the conversation, even though she hadn't wanted to. So had Craig. What surprised her was Craig going up to Jen and saying he would try and talk to Robert; Jen smiled gratefully.

It hadn't taken him long to catch up. Robert had been walking slowly and hadn't got very far. He also hadn't been paying attention to where he was going and tripped over a raised crack in the footpath. Craig had grabbed his arm before he fell. They walked in silence for a while before Craig raised the subject, which Robert hadn't responded well to, initially telling

Craig to stop sounding like Jen. But Craig persisted, and eventually, Robert admitted that he needed to find the stop button.

When Craig came back he told Andie what happened. Andie felt good about what Craig had done. She just wished it had been enough. But it wasn't.

The following day, they headed off early, ready to cross the border into Victoria, with the first stop being Bendigo.

'Guess we should do some more mining-related activities,' Craig said after they arrived.

Andie nodded. 'But I think this will be very different to what we've done before. This looks very touristy.'

'Even so,' Craig said. 'This was a gold rush town in the 1850s, so we should do something related to gold mining.'

'I'm happy to see some of the mining history, but I'm not going underground again,' Jen said.

'Are you still going on about that?' Robert said, his earlier apology clearly forgotten. 'You'll be fine.'

Jen turned and scowled at Robert. This was enough to stop him from saying anything more.

'I don't mind staying above ground with you,' Andie said. 'One underground mine tour is enough for me.'

So, the women stayed above ground and found a coffee shop that served Devonshire tea while Craig and Robert went sixty-one metres underground at the Central Deborah Gold Mine.

'I haven't had one of these in a long time,' Jen said.

Andie shook her head. 'Me either. I'd forgotten how good they are.'

They ate their scones with jam and cream in silence for a while. There was something about the way Jen looked that made Andie think she needed some quiet time. So, she waited until Jen was happy to start a conversation.

'I can't believe how long we've been going and how much we've seen.'

Andie nodded. 'I'm glad you've been taking photos. I'll never remember everything otherwise.'

Andie thought about the photos she'd taken and realised there weren't many of her and Craig together. Of course, that hadn't been deliberate. But it was telling all the same.

'Thanks for staying above ground with me. I'm still scarred from the last one.'

'That's all right. I didn't need to do another one, and the guys have gone together.'

Jen nodded. 'Yes, that should keep Robert out of trouble for a while. No alcohol down there.'

'Has he said anything more?'

Jen shook her head. 'He won't talk about it, and I'm out of ideas of what I can do to help. At least Craig had some success talking to him.'

For the next five minutes, they drank their coffee in silence. Andie didn't know what to do to help either. Eventually, Jen started speaking again. But she didn't want to talk about Robert's drinking. So, they talked about what they planned to see in Victoria and Tasmania, which, according to their itinerary, should take them to the end of October. When the guys returned, they all walked around town until late afternoon. Then they got in their cars and headed the 119 kilometres to Ballarat. Jen suggested staying at the caravan park and having a BBQ for dinner, and Andie agreed with her before either of the guys could have a say. Jen locked away the wine Robert had bought in a storage cupboard and kept the key. He wasn't happy when he realised he'd be having a dry night, but Jen wouldn't let him have the key, and for once, Craig agreed. The next morning, even Robert had to admit that he felt better than he had in a long time.

Ballarat

Today we visited Sovereign Hill, which, according to the website, brings to life the excitement of the gold rushes of the 1850s. We had fun walking through the town and seeing what it would have looked like in its heyday.

We panned for gold, watched some street theatre, and took photos of the characters walking around in costumes. We watched blacksmiths at work and gold being poured, and we were all tempted by what was in the confectionery factory.

'I'm glad we went there,' Jen said later that afternoon after the blog entry had been completed. 'Shall we make plans for dinner?'

Andie consulted her phone for restaurants in the area. 'The Yacht Club might be nice. It's right on the water.'

Andie liked the idea of sitting by the water, watching the sunset, and hopefully, having time to think. Even though she'd decided her future, lately, she'd been wavering. Was she really doing the right thing?

When they arrived, they were lucky enough to get a table right next to the window. The sun was still an hour away from setting, so they had plenty of time to settle. Craig and Robert went to the bar, and Jen went to the bathroom. As Andie sat alone at their table, she looked out the window at the sailing boats and thought again about getting a boat of her own. Maybe it was something she could do when she got home. Wherever that might be.

'Here you go,' Craig said as he handed Andie a drink.

She thanked him and went back to looking out the window. Behind her, she could hear the others talking, but she was more interested in looking at the water. The gentle, blue ripples were helping to push away all other thoughts. Except for the one she needed to think about. Were her wavering thoughts a result of being scared of what the future might hold? Or was she making the wrong decision?

'Earth to Andie,' Jen said.

'Sorry, distracted by the view.'

'It is beautiful. Wouldn't it be lovely to live somewhere with a view like this?'

Andie nodded. 'Or a view of the ocean. That would be lovely too.'

As she said it, she wondered if there was somewhere she could buy a house with an ocean view that she could afford.

'So, we're off to Melbourne tomorrow,' Robert said, sipping his soft drink. 'I'm looking forward to that. Maybe we could see a show while we're there.'

'Or a sporting event,' Craig said.

Jen turned to look at Andie. 'I get the feeling we might be going to different events.'

Andie shook her head. 'I'm not going to a sporting event.'

'Even if it's at the MCG?' Craig asked.

Andie thought about it. 'I guess that's different. The atmosphere would be good.'

'And there are some great shops near the MCG,' Jen said.

'Trust you to know that,' Craig said.

'Of course. I've been to Melbourne plenty of times, and unlike other cities, I've occasionally had some free time. There are a lot of places I know of that we can go to.'

'We don't need ideas about where to go shopping,' Craig said.

'She doesn't shop that much,' Robert said. 'She's been there enough to know the city well, not just the shops.'

'How about we order dinner now,' Andie said. 'Jen can tell us about some things we should do in Melbourne while we eat.'

After their meals arrived, Jen ran through some things she thought they'd enjoy. The more she spoke, the less sceptical Craig looked. About time he realised that Jen was interested in more than just shopping Andie thought. And she was pleased that Robert stuck to soft drink. For Jen's sake as well as his own.

'I guess this means we're back in civilisation,' Robert said to Jen as they came to a standstill on the Western Highway on their way into Melbourne.

Jen turned to look at him. 'We never left civilisation. It was just less crowded where we'd been. Anyway, you said the other day that you were starting to like the country.'

He nodded. 'Yes, just not the desert. It was kilometre after kilometre of nothing.'

'Which made it interesting because it's not what we're used to.'

'There's a reason we're not used to it.'

'Stop complaining. We're back in the city now. You should be happy.'

'We're not there yet. We're stuck in traffic on the outskirts.'

Jen sighed. She didn't want to talk anymore. All she could think about was how many bars and pubs were in Melbourne. One night of drinking soft drink wasn't enough to cure him.

They couldn't find a caravan park by the water in the middle of the city, so they picked the one closest to the CBD, which was only eleven kilometres away.

'Doesn't look like there's a lot around here,' Robert said.

Andie looked at him, thinking he was looking for a bar. But she didn't say it out loud.

'That's all right,' Jen said. 'We're only sleeping here. The rest of the time, we'll be out and about, exploring the city.'

'What shall we do first?' Andie said.

'Let's head into the city centre,' Jen said. 'There's a free tram that does a loop, and you can see some of the sites.'

Andie nodded. 'Sounds good. Do we catch a train in from here?'

Jen nodded and then started to speak before Robert interrupted. 'Can't we get a taxi? I don't want to sit in some grotty train carriage.'

Jen shook her head. 'It's not all about you. We're catching a train.'

Andie smiled and mouthed a thank you in Jen's direction. She and Craig were already over their budget again and needed to reign in the spending. As they walked to the train, Andie couldn't stop thinking about the budget, not just for the trip but the one after the trip. Could she afford everything on her own?

Melbourne

By the end of the day, we'd done the tram and wandered around Melbourne, getting an idea of the places we would come back to over the next few days. As usual, Craig was hungry, and Jen suggested we go to Lygon St for Italian. We'd been planning on looking at the sites as we sat on the tram on the way to dinner, but a minute after we hopped on, the unpredictable Melbourne weather kicked in, and it started raining—not just light rain, but a heavy downpour that obscured our view, more like a sudden summer storm than what we're used to seeing in September. But Melbourne being Melbourne, the weather changed, and the rain stopped as suddenly as it started. It didn't take long to find a restaurant we were all happy with.

Except Jen, the minute Robert went back on his promise and ordered a bottle of wine. Not something to be included in the blog, Andie thought. Thankfully, he kept his order to one bottle, which he shared. It was the least Andie had seen Robert drink in a long time, and when the bottle was gone, he didn't order another one.

The same couldn't be said for the following night after they returned from their day trip to the Great Ocean Road to see the Twelve Apostles. Over dinner, while discussing the next day's excursion to see the fairy penguins, Robert ordered a second bottle of wine with dinner. Something Andie didn't include in the blog later that night.

Great Ocean Road

It was amazing to see the Twelve Apostles, the limestone stacks jutting out of the ocean along the coastline. It's estimated they were formed over 10 to 20 million years. We could have stayed longer at the lookout, but it was extremely windy, and we could only stand there for a short time.

While we were in the vicinity, we left the lookout and wandered around Lorne, which, even though it's the largest town on the Great Ocean Road, is relatively small. But it was picturesque, and our trip to Erskine Falls was a highlight.

While out and about today, we also called in at Torquay and Bells Beach. Thanks to the weather, it was too cold to swim in either location, although, even if it had been warm enough, the ocean looked more suited to surfing than a gentle paddle.

The next morning, Robert wanted bacon and eggs for breakfast.

'We don't have time to cook,' Jen said. 'You'll have to eat cereal. Otherwise, we'll have to get you something on the way.'

Robert opened his mouth to speak, but a glance at Jen stopped him.

'How far do we have to go?' Craig asked.

'It's about 140 kilometres to Phillip Island,' Jen said.

'That's where they have the motorcycle grand prix,' Craig said.

Jen smiled. 'But not at this time of year. We're off to see the penguins.'

'I thought they came in at night,' Andie said.

Jen nodded. 'They do, but if we're going to drive for ninety minutes to get to Phillip Island, we may as well see everything else on the island.'

During the drive, Robert was quiet. Jen knew he wasn't feeling well. Not even the greasy breakfast they'd stopped to buy him on the way helped. But she had to put those thoughts out of her mind. Yes, he'd gone against what he'd said, but she knew him well enough to know that he would try again. And she also knew that it would likely take several attempts at trying again.

As she glanced at him out of the corner of her eye, she realised that despite everything, she wanted things to work out. She just didn't know if they would.

Phillip Island

At dusk, we took our seats to wait for the penguins. We were tired after the drive and exploring the island, but we were all keen to see them—even Robert, who hadn't been that keen. And eventually, they arrived, waddling up along the beach. They were adorable, and we couldn't take our eyes off them. And Jen couldn't stop taking photos, as you can see by this blog entry.

It was definitely worth the drive, and it was a fitting last thing to see before we leave Victoria tomorrow and head to Tasmania.

And seeing something as cute as the penguins was exactly what Andie needed as it pushed her troubles from her mind. But only for a little while.

Chapter Fourteen

'I hope the crossing is calm,' Jen said as she looked out over Bass Straight. 'I hate rough seas.'

Andie nodded. 'Me too.'

The calmer, the better, Andie thought. And her desire for calm extended beyond the ocean.

'I'm looking forward to this,' Jen said. 'Tassie is meant to be beautiful.'

'I've heard that the west coast is spectacular,' Andie said.

Jen nodded. 'I've heard that too. And even Robert is excited to go there.'

Andie hesitated for a moment before speaking. 'He seems to be drinking less lately.'

'Hopefully, it's a step in the right direction,' Jennifer said, although she didn't look convinced.

Andie squeezed her hand, and they went inside to find Craig and Robert. And saw that Jen was right not to be convinced when they found them at the bar.

'I told Craig not to go to the bar with Robert,' Andie said, frustrated.

'You don't have to do that. It's not Craig's problem.'

'He's not helping though.'

'There you are,' Craig said when they arrived at the table.

'We went for a walk around the deck,' Andie said. 'You should try it instead of sitting here.'

'I'm quite happy sitting here,' Robert said. 'What about you, Craig?'

Craig nodded. 'Ok with me.'

'Great. I'll go and get us another round.'

Andie waited until Robert had left the table. 'What are you doing?'

Craig looked at her. 'What?'

'You're not supposed to be encouraging him to drink.'

Craig put his beer down. 'I forgot about that.'

'Why am I not surprised? But you only spoke with him recently.'

'This will be the last one. We'll go for a walk on the deck after that.'

Jen hadn't said anything, and Craig deliberately looked away from her.

How could Craig be so stupid, Andie thought as she got up from the table and walked away. When she got to the door, she turned around but neither of them noticed her. As she stood outside on the deck, all she could see was the ocean. Dark blue and uninviting. No other boats. It was cold, and there was no one else outside. She was on her own. Would it be that different if she really was?

Early the next morning, as they prepared to disembark, Andie noticed that Jen and Robert weren't talking to each other. Even Craig noticed the tension between them.

'He really does have a problem, doesn't he?'

Andie sighed to herself. Was it that hard for him to understand? She didn't say that aloud. Instead, she told him, again, not to do anything to encourage Robert.

'I won't. Wouldn't hurt me to cut back anyway.'

After disembarking, they drove to the caravan park they'd booked in Devonport, set up and then headed out to explore. Jen and Robert still weren't speaking. They planned to stay in town for two days, using the second to do a day trip to Cradle Mountain. But first, Devonport. One of the things Andie wanted to see while they were there was the Tasmanian Arboretum, which was the last thing on their itinerary for the day.

As they walked around, Andie found herself separated from the others. She thought about trying to find them but being alone felt right. The trees were comforting, tall, strong, and still, and the colours were a feast for her eyes.

She strolled through the gardens, taking it all in. Just ahead of her was an older couple. They were standing in front of a Southern Hemisphere Conifer, reading the information about the tree, holding hands. Andie knew that would never be her and Craig.

The following morning, they got up early. It was a ninety-minute drive to Cradle Mountain, and they wanted to give themselves as much time there as possible. They'd all heard the weather could be unpredictable, and there was a high chance they could get there and not see the mountain because of fog or heavy rain.

Which was exactly the case when they arrived. The fog was so thick they could barely see in front of them.

'I think it's up there somewhere,' Jen said, pointing to her left.

Andie turned to where Jen was pointing, although considering she couldn't see anything, she wasn't sure why she did. 'I hope the weather changes. I'd really like to see it, and this is our only chance.'

'Let's start walking, and hopefully, as we get closer, we'll see something,' Jen said.

Craig wasn't happy about another walk, but he wanted to see the mountain. Andie hadn't told him they planned on doing the two-hour walk. He'd find out soon enough, and by then, they'd be far enough along the path that there would be no point turning back.

As they walked, Andie was fascinated by the grasslands, rainforests and ancient plants. She was hoping they'd see a Tasmanian devil too. They'd been walking for about an hour when the fog started to lift, and the sun came peeking through the clouds.

'There it is,' Jen said.

They all turned where she was pointing, and they could finally see the mountain with its twin peaks and plunging hollow in between.

As Jen took photos, Andie was content to just look at it, giving her a sense of peace. Last night she'd started wavering again, thinking about her future. So many times, she'd been certain of the path she needed to take. And then, occasionally, she changed her mind. Staring at the mountain, she hoped to quieten the chatter in her mind once and for all.

Cradle Mountain

We were so lucky today that we got to see Cradle Mountain, as not everyone who visits does because of the

*weather. At 1,545 metres above sea level, and with the clouds
floating around the summit, it looked like the mountain was
almost touching the sky. Located in the heart of the Tasmanian
Wilderness Area, it has the sort of natural beauty that you should
see for yourself. Descriptions don't do it justice, and photos
can't capture the feeling of what it's like to be there.*

*We wanted to see a Tasmanian Devil but didn't spot any.
We did, however, spot several wombats and a platypus. There
are plenty of walking tracks, and we headed along a couple of
them but stayed away from the longest, an 80-kilometre track
that is a five-to-six-day hike from Cradle Mountain to Lake St
Clair. None of us would contemplate doing that!*

After Andie had finished typing, while Jen was
uploading photos, she realised that Robert hadn't complained
about any of the walks. In fact, he'd actually looked like he'd
enjoyed them.

That night they were all tired, so they stayed at the
caravan park. Andie had been waiting for Robert to suggest a
restaurant. And for Jen not to be happy about it. But he was the
one who suggested they stay in. And Andie was even more
surprised when Robert drank water. Even when they got back in
the afternoon, a time when Robert was the first to reach for a
drink, he didn't. No words were spoken, but by silent agreement,

the others stuck to water too. They could all tell Robert noticed, but he didn't say anything. The next morning Jen looked happier than she had in a long time.

As they drove the hour and twenty minutes from Devonport to Launceston, Andie didn't speak. Instead, she concentrated on the countryside, so lush and green. It reminded her of parts of New Zealand she and Craig had visited several years before. It had been one of the few trips she'd managed to talk him into.

Not long after arriving in Launceston, they headed off to the Cataract Gorge cruise they'd booked.

'As well as the cruise, there's gardens, bushland, a suspension bridge, lots of views and the world's longest single-span chairlift that goes across the gorge,' Jen said.

'The chairlift sounds good,' Robert said, smiling at Jen. 'We should go on that.'

Jen nodded and smiled back.

That afternoon, Andie was happy. As well as enjoying everything they'd done at the gorge, Jen and Robert had held hands for most of the day. Even with the emotions churning through her mind, she was pleased for them. When they arrived back at the caravan park, they picked up a tourist brochure from the office, sat down and went through it. There was plenty to do while they were there and a lot in the surrounding area, including a wine tour in the Tamar Valley. Andie held her breath, but to her surprise, Robert flicked the page over and continued. He didn't mention wanting to go, and no one else brought it up, even though the valley was meant to be beautiful. And the smile that had been on Jen's face most of the day was there again.

Tasmania – the next few days

Our itinerary has been decided. First, we're going to drive over to St Helens, visiting the Bay of Fires, then follow the road down to St Mary's, Bicheno and the Freycinet Peninsula. From there, we'll drive to the town of Richmond and then on to Hobart.

Bay of Fires

First stop, the Bay of Fires. We were all intrigued by how the place got its name, so this time, I got in first with the research. There are two possible explanations. It could be related to the bright orange lichen that grows on the granite boulders, or it could be related to some Aboriginal fires that Captain Tobias Furneaux spotted when he sailed past in 1773. However it got its name, it's beautiful. The crystal-clear water and white sandy beach are stunning.

St Helens

Second stop, St Helens. It's the largest town on the northeast coast of Tasmania and where we are spending the night. The town is the second largest fishing port in Tasmania, something we were very happy about when we had dinner. Particularly the lobster!

We had an interesting conversation with some locals sitting at the table next to ours. We asked what we would find in St Marys, the next town on our itinerary. In response, we were told they'd never been there, so couldn't tell us. It was too far for them to go. But it's only thirty minutes from St Helens to St Marys! Guess they have a different idea about distance than we do.

Andie looked back at what she'd written the night before about their itinerary and then at the entry she'd just finished. She left out the part where Robert ordered a drink to go with his dinner, followed by another one. And the look on Jen's face when she saw him do it. She and Andie hadn't drunk, and Craig had sat on the same beer the whole time they were there.

The next morning, Robert looked worse for wear. Andie could only assume he'd continued drinking when he got back to the caravan. Jen got behind the wheel. She didn't say anything to Robert. Considering what was going on with both couples, Andie thought it was an omen that they were ahead of their schedule. And that no one had mentioned anything about that. At the rate they were going, they'd be finished in ten months, not twelve. Which was probably a good thing.

St Mary's was only a small town, but it was pretty. Robert stayed in the car, fast asleep in his seat. Jen walked around town without speaking. Craig tried to talk to Andie, but she wasn't in the mood to talk either. Robert woke up when they came back, and Jen started their car. Andie could see through the window that Jen didn't reply when Robert started talking. She didn't say anything to him when they pulled up in Bicheno either. She only spoke after they set up the caravans and started talking about tomorrow's trip to the Freycinet Peninsula.

'You can't give up so easily.'

'I know.'

'Do you understand what you're doing to us?' Jen said, feeling sadder than she let on.

Andie didn't hear anymore. She walked away so they could be alone.

'How stunning,' Jen said as she looked out at Wineglass Bay the next morning.

Andie nodded as she stood beside her, happy that Jen had something to distract her from Robert.

'There's a boat,' Jen said, indicating to their right. 'It would be great to go out on the water. Should we find out where it goes from?'

Andie nodded. She wouldn't worry about the budget today. Jen had enough going on. So did Andie.

Out on the boat, the water looked even more like glass. It was so beautiful that Andie's thoughts went back to living near the ocean and getting a boat of her own.

The following day, just outside of Hobart, they stopped in Richmond.

'Why are we stopping here?' Craig said. 'I know you told me, but I've forgotten.'

Andie sighed. 'We're stopping because it's a beautiful town with a lot of history and lots to see.'

Craig wasn't convinced, but he got out of the car anyway. 'Where to first?'

'We're going to look at a church.'

This information didn't increase his enthusiasm. But Andie was interested in history, so they walked inside the oldest Catholic Church in Australia. And from there, it was on to the most photographed spot in Richmond—Richmond Bridge, the oldest sandstone bridge still in use anywhere in the country. Jen was focused on taking her usual number of photos, which is why it took her a minute to register what Robert said.

'There are some good wineries around here.'

No one said anything. The look on Jen's face meant no one had to. She said nothing on the way back to the car and the rest of the journey into Hobart.

'What is wrong with him?' she said to Andie later that day after they'd arrived in Hobart.

Andie shrugged. What could she say? Except that maybe Jen thought it would be easier for Robert to change than it was. She kept that information to herself though.

Later that night, Andie could hear them arguing. She didn't want to, but their caravan was close by. Craig was asleep beside her and didn't hear a thing. When he woke up, she wouldn't be telling him that she'd heard Jen say that if Robert didn't get his act together, she didn't know if she could stay with him.

The next day Jen and Robert were barely speaking to each other. As the four of them walked around the Salamanca markets, Andie and Craig could feel the tension between the other two. By the time they reached the end, Andie had realised that Jen hadn't bought anything. She'd barely looked at anything either. Andie decided that maybe the two of them should spend the afternoon together. But Jen didn't want to change their plans, so the four of them went to the top of Mt Wellington to look at the view of the city and the ocean. Craig didn't complain when they went on the walking tracks. And Robert didn't say a word all afternoon.

That night, Andie didn't write a blog entry. She didn't think Jen would want to be reminded of that day. And for the first time on the trip, Jen hadn't taken a single photo.

'I hope they're not like that tomorrow,' Craig said as they were getting into bed that night.

Andie nodded. 'Me too.'

She watched him as he fell asleep and wondered how he'd react when she finally told him. Based on what she saw from Jen and Robert that day, she would have to keep her decision to herself until the end of the trip. Or as close to the end as she could. And not for the first time, she was glad that Craig was so bad at picking up on how she was feeling.

On the drive to Port Arthur the next day, Jen and Robert were quiet. Even Andie running through the information about their destination didn't elicit much response from either of them. So, after she'd finished reading, she turned her attention to what was outside the window and looked at the scenery and the towns they went through on the way. It took them just over an hour and a half to get to their destination, and Andie was glad when they finally arrived and they could all get out of the car.

They paid their entry fee, looked at a map and then headed in. They hadn't got very far before seeing the remains of the Broad Arrow Café and the memorial created for the victims of the massacre in 1996. Jen read the names of the victims on the plaque and thought about all those families who would still be grieving over those they lost, and she realised that being angry with Robert wouldn't achieve anything. She needed to go about things a different way.

As they walked through the grounds, looking at the ruins of the prison, reading about how the convicts lived, how they were treated and how many lashes they received when they tried to escape, her thoughts turned more and more to finding a solution. She didn't have to think very long, though, as Robert brought up the subject. They were standing outside one of the prison buildings looking out to the sea when he started talking. Andie and Craig were still inside, looking at the jail cells.

'I need to do something about my drinking.'

Jen nodded. She didn't say anything because she wanted him to keep talking.

'Something about this place made me realise. Drinking is something I can't seem to escape from.'

Jen took his hand. 'But you can if you want to.'

'Not by myself.'

'You're not by yourself. You have me. And you have Andie and Craig. And if we need to, we can get professional help.'

Robert looked at her, a shocked look on his face. 'I'm not that bad.'

Jen saw the look and let that suggestion drop. She could always bring it up again if needed. 'Ok, let's see how we go together.'

That was the end of the conversation as Andie and Craig came out to join them. But Jen would tell them. The more people that were helping him, the more chance of success, she thought.

Port Arthur

Port Arthur is a world heritage site, one of the few remaining examples of penal colonies from the 18th and 19th centuries. For twenty years, from 1833 to 1853, Port Arthur was where those who were deemed hardened criminals in Britain were transported to serve their sentences. Conditions were harsh, and many tried to escape, although very few did so successfully.

We toured the remains of the jail cells and saw where convicts were tied up before receiving the nominated number of lashes doled out as punishments. We also saw the wild ocean on

the edge of the site, the reason why few prisoners escaped.
Between drowning and sharks, it wasn't a good option.

We spent most of the day there before heading back to
Hobart, stopping in a few small towns on the way.

Andie read what she'd written once more, closed the
laptop and got ready for dinner.

That night, they found a restaurant in Salamanca that had a cosy
feel. They were seated at a table at the back where it was quiet.
The dim lighting added to the ambience but made it hard to read
the menu. The wine list was placed in front of Robert, but he
didn't pick it up.

'Too dark to read it,' he said.

'I can give you some recommendations,' the waiter said.

Robert shook his head. 'That's ok. I'm happy with
water.'

Andie and Craig looked at each other but didn't say
anything. They told the waiter they were happy to stick with
water too. Jen smiled at them and mouthed thank you.

'You don't have to stick with water if you don't want
to,' Robert said.

'I don't mind,' Andie said.

Craig nodded. 'Me either.'

'But you're not the one with the problem. I am.'

No one said anything for a moment until Jen broke the silence. 'We had a conversation this afternoon, and Robert wants to stop drinking.'

'That's great,' Andie said. 'I'm glad you've made the decision.'

'Is it that obvious that I have a problem?'

Andie nodded. 'Not at first, but it became more obvious the longer we've been on this trip.'

'Well, I've said it now, so I'm going to do something about it.'

'I'm happy not to drink in support,' Andie said.

Craig nodded. 'Me too.'

Jen reached over and grabbed their hands. 'Thank you.'

'You don't have to do that,' Robert said.

'We know,' Andie said. 'But we want to.'

'So that's the end of that discussion,' Craig said. 'Let's order food.'

They spent dinner talking about the places they'd be visiting during the rest of their stay in Tasmania. No one mentioned alcohol again.

Strahan

This morning we headed northwest. The road was winding, and it took us longer to get to Strahan than we thought it would. We stopped for a few quick breaks but wanted to keep driving so we could get there. We're planning to stay two days and use one of the days to do a cruise on the Franklin River.

Andie was looking forward to the peace and quiet and the chance to see some beautiful scenery, hoping it would distract her enough to keep her thoughts at bay.

When we arrived in Strahan, we were pleased to see how nice the caravan park was. We hadn't been sure what we would find in a town of around six hundred and fifty people, but we'd forgotten how popular it was with tourists. As we looked around, we were sure there were more tourists than locals, and we wondered if the locals ever got annoyed or did they realise how dependent they were on tourists for their livelihoods.

Either way, living in a town like this wasn't something Andie thought she could do long-term. She would need somewhere with fewer visitors intruding.

After setting up, we headed to the marina and picked a boat for tomorrow. It was getting dark by the time we were done, so we started to think about dinner. None of us felt like cooking after the winding and often slow drive, but we all wanted to stay outside. Robert spotted the fish and chip shop and suggested we get takeaway and eat it by the water. And it was here that we tried a Tasmanian delicacy we'd heard about—scallop pies. We hadn't tried them because we weren't sure about seafood in a pie. It just sounded odd. But we were wrong. They were delicious. That's something great about this trip—trying new things.

As they boarded the boat the following day, the first thing they saw was a bar.

'Drinks are included with lunch,' the crew member told them.

Jen looked at the bar. 'I didn't see that mentioned when we booked.'

Andie shook her head. 'Me either.'

Jen went to find a seat, a worried look on her face. Andie followed her.

'It will be fine. He's done ok the past few days.'

Jen nodded, but Andie could tell she didn't believe her.

The cruise left the dock, and for the next few hours, they were all spellbound by the wilderness around them. Even Jen stopped thinking about Robert and looked happy. Until she realised that she didn't know where he'd gone. She wandered around the boat until she found him sitting with some overseas tourists in the back corner on the upper deck. With a glass of wine in his hand. Jen took one look at him, turned around and walked away. Robert put the glass down and followed her.

'It was only one,' he said.

'I don't care. It was meant to be none.'

Jen went back to the lower deck and told him not to follow her. She didn't want to see him. She wanted to be alone. Robert watched her go.

'It was bound to happen,' Andie said after she found Jen.

'He promised me he wouldn't.'

Andie nodded. 'I know, but I think it's harder for him than any of us realise.'

'I suppose.'

'Try not to be too hard on him. He is trying. We just need to keep supporting him.'

Jen nodded. 'You're right. I'm just disappointed in him.'

'I know, but he'll get there.'

'Will he?'

Andie nodded. 'He wants to, so I think he will.'

Jen squeezed Andie's hand. 'Thanks.'

After the cruise, Jen and Robert had a long talk, and things seemed to be ok between them. For the rest of their time in Tasmania, Robert didn't touch a drop of alcohol. And Jen realised that no matter what, she wanted them to stay together.

Chapter Fifteen

Disembarking in Victoria, they started on the journey north to New South Wales, arriving at the beginning of November. Once they got there, it would be the last state of their trip. Andie couldn't believe how quickly the time had gone. No matter what her life would become after this, the past eight months were something she'd never forget. The people they'd met, the places they'd been and the experiences they'd had—good and bad.

'Where's our first stop?' Jen asked.

'Lakes Entrance,' Andie said. 'It's 380 kilometres from here and looks like a lovely spot to stay.'

Andie hoped it was as tranquil as some of the descriptions she'd read made it out to be. As much for Robert as for her. The past few days had been hard for him, but to his credit, he hadn't given in. Jen had discretely mentioned that he'd been talking with someone online, someone used to helping people with the same issue he was dealing with. He'd only had two sessions, but it was a step in the right direction. Andie wondered if she should talk to someone. She and Craig had spent so many years together. Moving on would be hard.

For some reason, their first date had popped into her mind the day before. It hadn't been anything fancy, not back in high school. They'd gone to the movies. Neither of them could remember what movie they had seen. Craig had picked her up. He'd only just got his licence and was so proud when he pulled up on her driveway and got out of the car. That feeling changed when her dad answered the door. Andie's dad was a tall man with broad shoulders, and if you didn't know him, which Craig didn't, he could look intimidating. But he was a quiet, considered man, which Craig eventually found out. But that day, all Craig could see was his size. Andie had introduced them, and her dad invited Craig inside. Andie could see him shaking, no matter how much he tried to hide it. It was lucky for Craig that her mum had been working. She'd been a nurse all her working life and had been on night shift the week of their first date. She would have asked Craig lots of questions. As it was, her dad only asked a few and then told them to have a good night.

Craig had opened the car door for her, which at the time, made her feel very grown up. He'd driven them to the cinemas, and Andie could see how hard he was concentrating on his driving. They hardly spoke, neither of them sure what to say. During the movie, he'd reached over and taken hold of her hand. At the end of the night, they'd kissed. It had been clumsy and awkward, neither of them knowing what they were doing. But it had still been nice, a small step towards growing up. And after that, there had been another date, then one after that and then another and another. They dated throughout grade twelve, and come formal time, there was no question who either of them would go with. Andie remembered how handsome Craig had looked in his black suit. It was the first time since they'd been together that he'd worn a suit. He'd also worn a purple tie to match her dress. They still had the photos somewhere. They'd gone with some of their friends in a limo, and there was a photo of them standing next to it before they got in. They had been trying to look sophisticated but couldn't hide their excitement. At the end of the night, after the dancing, speeches, and after-formal party, Craig told her they would be together forever. But after school, his prediction didn't come true for that brief time when they were apart. Just like it wouldn't come true now.

After school, they both changed. Craig went into his apprenticeship, and she started her teaching degree. Suddenly her world was about juggling study and work and friends. And Craig. While his apprenticeship was hard at times, when he finished for the day, that was it. When she got home, she still had assignments to complete and exams to study for. Craig wanted to go out and would get annoyed when she said she couldn't. And the people she met at university came from all different backgrounds, and she learned so much through them; the discussions they had, even the new foods they introduced her to.

Craig spent his days on job sites with guys from the same background, ate food from hotboxes and looked forward to finishing at 2 pm on a Friday so they could go to the pub. He didn't understand her world, and she didn't understand his. After a while, it became too much of a gap between them. She still thought of him when they were apart, more out of missing something familiar, something that had been part of her life. When she saw him again, initially, she'd been unsure about starting again, but something in the back of her mind told her she should. From there, they followed a traditional path—a few more years of dating, an engagement, a house and a wedding. But tradition stopped there. Even though they'd built a house with extra bedrooms, there was never anyone to fill them, despite the many attempts. So, they settled into their reality, and life continued. She couldn't say it was a particularly exciting life, but she'd been content. Or at least she thought she had. Now she realised she'd just settled. And it wasn't enough anymore.

The night they spent in Lakes Entrance passed without any drama. Andie kept her emotions in check, and Robert didn't drink. She would have liked to spend more time there because it was a beautiful place, but when the subject came up, she was the one who said they should move on. She didn't know how much longer she could keep quiet and didn't want to add an extra night to their trip. So early the next morning, they headed to the nation's capital, Canberra. Robert hadn't been excited because everything he'd heard about the place didn't give him any confidence that it was worth the drive.

'It's full of politicians,' he said.

They all agreed that was enough not to bother going, but it was the capital, so they thought they should. If nothing else, Andie was interested in seeing the war memorial. Both her grandfathers had fought in the Second World War, and she was interested to learn more about what it had been like for the Australians who fought. The first thing though, when they arrived, was to find a caravan park.

'Have we been driving around in circles for the past twenty minutes?' Craig asked.

Andie nodded. 'I think so.'

'How do we get off this road?'

Andie shrugged.

'I'm taking the first exit I see.'

'Ok, I'll text Jen and let her know.'

Thank goodness she texted back. *Robert's getting annoyed.*

They eventually found a caravan park, and it didn't matter that it wasn't the one they'd seen online and had planned to stay at. They just wanted to pull up somewhere.

'It's freezing,' Jen said when they got out of the cars.

Andie nodded. 'Let's set up then find a café and have a coffee.'

'Sounds good. Let's leave the guys here, and just the two of us go.'

Andie nodded. 'If you want.'

Twenty minutes later, they were seated in a café only a few doors down from the caravan park.

'Ok, what's going on?' Jen said.

Andie looked up from her coffee. 'What do you mean?'

'You haven't been yourself lately. I know something is happening.'

Andie didn't say anything for a moment. 'Do you think the guys have noticed?'

Jen shook her head. 'You'd need to have something written in big letters on a billboard for them to notice anything.'

Andie smiled for the first time in a little while. And then she told Jen that she didn't want to be with Craig anymore.

'Wow. I don't know what to say.'

'Me either.'

'How long have you been thinking about this?'

'Almost from the start of the trip.'

'You've hidden it well then.'

'I should get an acting award.'

Jen smiled and leaned over and squeezed Andie's hand. 'I don't think there is an award for that.'

'I know.'

'When are you going to tell him?'

Andie shrugged. 'I keep thinking I should leave it until the end of the trip, but I'm not sure how much longer I can keep pretending. It's getting harder each day.'

They spent the rest of the time sitting in silence until they'd finished their coffees. There wasn't anything else to say.

That afternoon, they started sightseeing around Canberra, but Andie didn't take much of it in. She was too preoccupied because of her conversation with Jen. It was out in the open now, and she couldn't take it back. She knew Jen wouldn't say anything, even to Robert. It didn't matter though. He'd find out soon enough anyway.

The next morning, as they headed out, there was a chill in the air, even though it was the end of spring. Behind her, she could hear the others planning their day in Canberra. Robert made a joke about it being a day of nationals – National Gallery, National Museum, and National Library. Andie was looking forward to those places. She'd never been to any of them. Craig had never been one for culture. The only place he wanted to visit was the Australian War Memorial.

Andie ignored Craig's grumbling as they walked around the National Gallery. There was an Impressionist exhibition from London, and Andie enjoyed every minute. She could hear Jen and Robert talking in detail about the paintings they were looking at. She could have joined in, but she was content just looking at each one, admiring the colours and the skill involved in their creation. Then, a thought began to form in the back of her mind. A thought about seeing more paintings like these. In other galleries. In Europe. Somewhere she'd always wanted to go, but Craig had no interest. But the more Andie thought about it, the more she realised she could go on her own.

As they walked out of the gallery, Jen looked over at the National Portrait Gallery and saw a sign for an exhibition about love. She announced she wanted to go and walked over. They all followed except Craig. He said one gallery was enough, and he'd do something else. Andie watched him walk away as she stood at the entrance, the paintings and photos depicting love just behind her.

She didn't feel like looking at the pictures with Jen and Robert. They'd only been in the gallery five minutes, and they were already holding hands. She pretended to be interested in the picture she was looking at, even though it didn't capture her attention, and let them walk ahead. The more she saw the exhibition, the more she wondered why she'd agreed to see it. All the pictures celebrated love, which, the more she looked at, the more it became clear to her that she hadn't loved Craig for a long time.

That night at dinner, in a restaurant next to a wine bar, which Robert ignored, Andie was quiet. So much so that even

Robert said something. Not Craig, though. Andie told Robert she was tired, which wasn't far from the truth. She didn't clarify that it was emotional, not physical tiredness. The pictures only solidified her decision.

The next day started with a walk around Lake Burley Griffin. Craig grumbled about getting up early and then about how long the walk would take. Andie didn't acknowledge him. After all the time they'd spent in their cars since their journey began, any opportunity to walk was something she wouldn't miss. As she looked out over the lake, she could see kayakers gliding across the water in the early morning light. They looked so graceful. And peaceful. Andie wished she could find that feeling, even for a minute. But the calm of the lake, the light breeze that flowed around her, and the green of the park, made no difference. Today it wasn't her mind that was the cause. It was her heart. If a heart could be twisted into knots, then that's as close as she could get to describing how she felt. She was almost glad when they headed towards the war memorial. A few hours to focus on the displays would fill her thoughts. Giving the memorial anything less than her full attention would be disrespectful.

None of them had been to the war memorial before, even Jen, who'd travelled to Canberra for work several times. But like most of her work trips, there'd been no time for sightseeing. Andie thought it was interesting that she'd overheard Jen and

Robert talking about their careers and that maybe it was time for a change, time to slow down. Andie wasn't sure how serious they were. They'd worked so hard to get where they were. But Andie had noticed throughout their travels how much of their old selves had started to creep back in. Just small things here and there. She'd even heard Jen call him Rob a couple of times.

Craig was already behind them. He was never much of a reader; now, he stopped at every display and read every word of the descriptions. They were still in the first section, the First World War, the war to end all wars. Except that it wasn't. And only twenty-one years later, another generation went off to war, many of whom never returned. The further they walked through, the more Andie realised that no matter what was happening in her life, it was nothing compared to what happened to those who served.

At the end of the displays was the Hall of Remembrance with the long rows of names of those who didn't come back. Jen and Robert were looking for the names of relatives on the wall. Both of Andie's grandfathers came home, so there were no names for her to look for. Craig was still inside, still reading. And she was glad for the time to herself.

They left the memorial and decided to walk over to Civic, something Craig grumbled about. But Andie expected that. As with earlier that morning, she ignored him. Not far from their destination, they walked down a street full of public housing. As Andie looked at each house, she felt sad. None of the houses were looked after. There was graffiti over the walls, many windows were broken, and there was junk in most of the front yards. She only saw three residents on their walk, and all of them looked like they were under the influence of something, even though it was 1 pm.

But the sad feeling didn't last long. Even what she saw at the memorial started to fade as her troubles returned, and she hardly spoke for the rest of the afternoon. Even Craig noticed and asked her what was wrong, but she said nothing. Today was not the day.

Neither was the day after or the day after that, and soon they found themselves back on the New South Wales coast, and Andie hadn't said anything yet. And she hadn't written any blog entries while they'd been in Canberra. Her heart just wasn't in it. She wasn't sure if she'd do anymore. If anyone asked, she say she'd had enough of doing it, which wasn't far from the truth. Even though she'd loved writing it, anything she added now would feel like a lie. She certainly couldn't add the truth, especially after she finally told Craig.

They spent two weeks winding their way up to Sydney, stopping in some lovely beachside towns and enjoying the now early summer weather. With each stop, Andie knew the time was getting closer. By the time they got to Sydney, she knew she couldn't put it off any longer. She waited until they'd done their sightseeing; all the usual things—the Opera House, the Harbour Bridge, Bondi Beach, across to Manly on the ferry. There was no point ruining that for Craig. Even though she no longer wanted to be with him, she didn't want to hurt him. She knew there was no way that wouldn't happen, but if she could do anything to make it easier, she would.

The opportunity came on their last night in Sydney when Robert announced he was taking Jen out for a romantic dinner at one of the restaurants that lined the harbour. It was a small thank you for Jen putting up with him and everything he'd been going through. Craig didn't say anything and didn't suggest that he and Andie go somewhere. He was happy to have a BBQ at the caravan park.

'Not long until we're home,' Craig said.

Andie nodded.

'It will be good to get back to our own house and our own bed.'

Andie nodded again.

'And our lives can go back to how they were before we left.'

This time Andie shook her head. 'No, they can't.'

Craig turned to look at her. 'What do you mean?'

'I'm not happy, Craig. I can't do this anymore.'

'Do what?'

'Stay married.'

'What are you talking about?'

'I want a divorce.'

Craig looked at her for a minute, then turned around and walked off. She didn't see him again for two hours, and when he finally came back, he didn't say anything but went straight to bed. He didn't even look at her.

The following morning, he asked if she meant what she'd said the night before. Andie nodded and said she had.

'Are we going to finish the trip?'

Andie nodded again. 'If you want to.'

'You could have waited until we'd finished before telling me.'

'I know, but I just couldn't pretend anymore.'

He looked at her for a moment, then got up and went outside.

An hour later, he came back out. 'I'm going home. I don't want to continue. I've booked a flight leaving tonight. So you drive the car and caravan home.'

And then he left. Almost twenty-five years. Over so quickly.

Chapter Sixteen

After Craig left, Andie decided to drive straight back to
Brisbane. Jen and Robert wanted to continue with the planned
itinerary, but Andie couldn't. She drove as far as Newcastle with
them, hugging them both before she left, thanking them for being
part of the adventure. She planned to stop at Coffs Harbour, only
four hours away, but once she was on the road, she decided to
drive a bit further before stopping for the night. She saw the sign
for Yamba ninety minutes later and turned off the highway there.

The following day, when she got back to Brisbane, Craig wasn't
at the house. She'd sent him a message saying she was bringing
the car and caravan back, but he never responded. She couldn't
blame him. But she would have liked to see him. Talk to him.
The way things had ended. She felt like she needed to say more.
And that he should have an opportunity to say something too.

Andie moved in with her sister for a couple of weeks
while she decided what to do and where to go. Her last stop
before getting back to Brisbane had stayed in her mind.
Something about the town had appealed to her. So that was how
she found herself, six weeks after returning, sitting on a clifftop
in Yamba, staring out over the ocean.

Once she'd decided, it had only taken a week to find a
place to live and move her furniture. She was only renting at the
moment—she'd have to wait until the property settlement went

through before she could afford to buy anything. And she was in no hurry to do that. She'd seen Craig a few times before she'd moved. The first time she saw him after Sydney, he was angry; the second time, less so. By the third time, he admitted he had been feeling the same way. Things were still tense between them sometimes, but mostly it had been ok.

To her left was the Pacific Hotel, and she decided to walk down there and treat herself to lunch and a glass of wine. She'd had nothing to drink in the last part of the trip in support of Robert, but she didn't have to worry about that now. He was still in contact with the counsellor he'd been speaking to online, and so far, he was sticking to not drinking.

As she sat there sipping her wine, waiting for the food to come out, she could see dolphins swimming, a whole pod of them, so graceful and beautiful. Andie watched them until they were out of sight. After she'd eaten, she continued to sit for a while, taking in the view until she remembered all the unpacking she still needed to do. Before she left, she thought about the blog she'd written during the trip and how this spot would have made for a good entry. And it also reminded her of all the times during the trip that she and Jen had been focused on where they were and what they would do, rather than thinking about what was going on in their relationships.

Later that afternoon, she wished she hadn't been in such a hurry to unpack. She'd forgotten how exhausting it could be and how much thought she had to put into where things would go. Two more boxes, she said to herself. That's what she'd get through today, and then she'd do more tomorrow. She opened the first box she came to and then almost closed it again. It was the box of photos, cards, and other memories she'd collected over the years that she and Craig had been together. As she looked at the photos, she became teary. Even though this had been her idea, they'd still had a life together. She looked at the photo on top of the pile. It had been taken the year they'd both turned nineteen. They'd gone to Caloundra for the weekend. Just a small unit on a street back from the beach. They hadn't been able to afford anything right on the beach with an ocean view. The unit had been cramped and dark, but they'd had a great time. They spent the days at the beach, and at night, they got takeaway fish and chips and went back to the beach, sitting at a table in the park on the edge of the sand.

But the two people who laughed as they wiped the grease from the chips off their fingers as they sat looking at the ocean, a sea breeze blowing around them, no longer existed. Under the photos, she found a box containing the first piece of jewellery Craig bought her. A simple, plain gold bracelet. Since then, he'd bought her other things, more expensive things, although not for a long time. But the bracelet, even though it hadn't cost a lot, was the first piece of jewellery she'd received from a man. She took it out of the box and put it on. And she left it on for the next few days.

Three months after moving in, she was walking near the beach when she saw a small boat on a trailer parked on the side of the road with a for sale sign on it. She walked over and looked at it, picturing herself out on the water. She kept walking though. It was a silly idea. Even though she'd been thinking about it for a long time, she'd never had a boat. Why would she get one now? She'd need lessons, and how would she tow it? Her car didn't have a tow bar—she'd bought a new one and left the four-wheel drive with Craig. He was more likely to use it than she would, so she'd got a small sedan. Before she turned the corner though, she looked back one more time, stood for a moment, then shook her head and continued on.

Later that week, she went for another walk near the beach, using a different route this time. And halfway through her walk, she came across the boat. It still had the for sale sign on it. She looked closer at the sign this time. It had the price written on it, which Andie thought was reasonable, especially as the price included the trailer. Again, she walked on, but this time she took note of the owner's phone number. Just in case.

The following week, she came across the boat again, but this time in a new location. She pulled out her phone and rang the number. That afternoon, she met the current owner and, not long after, became the new owner. Now all she had to do was figure out how to take it out on the water.

A week later, the previous owner, Joe, rang to see how the boat was going. Andie confessed that it was still sitting on the trailer under the tarp she'd rigged up beside the carport. That phone call was how she found herself on the water the following day. Joe had taught many people over the years and was happy to teach Andie everything she needed to know about being a skipper. From the minute Andie got onboard, she loved it, and every day for the next twelve days, she was out on the water. When she finally finished her lessons, she organised for the test and was soon the owner of not only a boat but a boat licence too.

Four months after that, she also had a date. Joe had asked her out on the last day of her lessons, but she'd said no. She wasn't ready. But she kept running into him, and something made her change her mind the last time she'd seen him. So, she asked if he'd still like to go on that date. She hadn't been on a date in over twenty-five years, and it was an odd feeling. But Joe was lovely, and she felt at ease with him. She'd already spent so much time with him, and his patience while teaching her to drive the boat was something that had stood out for her. By the end of their lunch, she agreed to go out with him again. Jen rang later that afternoon, and even though she hadn't planned on telling her about the date, she found she couldn't keep it to herself.

'I need all the details,' she said. 'Tell me everything.'

So, Andie filled her in on how they met and their first date.

'He sounds lovely. I'm glad you agreed to go out with him again.'

'I did, but I'm having doubts.'

'Why?'

'Is it too soon?'

'Only you can know that. But if you had a good time at lunch, it can't hurt to have dinner with him and then see where it goes.'

After she hung up, Andie realised that Jen was right. She would go to dinner and then decide what to do from there.

Andie looked around the spare room one more time before walking out. The bed was made, two clean towels were sitting on the chair, the window was open to let in the fresh air, and she'd put two glasses in the room for water, one on each side of the bed. Then she checked her watch. If Jen and Robert had left when they said they were going to, they'd be here soon. They were her first visitors, and she was happy to be seeing them. She was also a little bit nervous. Not only were they her first visitors, but they were also the first people from her old life who were coming into her new life. And they were going to meet Joe. Jen would be ok, but she wasn't sure how Robert would react. As much as he and Craig were different, they'd bonded during the last part of the trip.

'Jen and Robert, this is Joe.'

'Nice to meet you, Joe. And please call me Rob.'

Andie turned around and looked at Jen. She shrugged and whispered that since they'd started their new business together, he was happy to be called Rob again.

Over dinner, Andie realised that she'd been worrying for nothing. Joe got on well with Jen and Rob, and the conversation flowed.

They all got up early the following morning to take the boat out.

'I can't believe what I'm seeing,' Jen said. 'Look at you go.'

Andie smiled as she launched the boat and started heading out slowly until they got away from the shore, and then she picked up speed. It was a beautiful day. The sun was shining and glistening on the calm, still water. A light breeze cooled things down, and everyone felt relaxed and happy. Rob and Joe continued talking at the back of the boat, and Jen stood by Andie at the front.

'You look like you're enjoying yourself.'

Andie nodded. 'I am. I should have done this years ago.'

'What, learn to drive a boat or start a new life?'

Andie paused for a moment before speaking. 'Both.'

'Well, you look happy. And I like Joe.'

'I'm glad. It means a lot.'

'And so does Rob.'

Andie smiled. 'Good.'

'He's been spending a lot of time with Craig. I hope you don't mind.'

'Why would I mind? Just because I needed to move on doesn't mean they can't spend time together.'

As they moored at the spot Andie had picked for them to go for a swim, she thought about Craig. She still cared for him and wished him nothing but happiness. It wasn't the life she wanted anymore, but he would always be special to her.

They swam for almost an hour and then went back to the shore to have a picnic, which Rob had put together. Ever since he'd left his job and started running their food truck business, he'd never been happier, and he spent a lot of time in the kitchen coming up with new dishes they could sell.

It hadn't taken long for Jen to give up her job after the end of the trip, either. She was hooked the first weekend she'd helped Rob out in their food truck. She loved how busy it was and how nice it was to talk to the customers. Soon they bought another one. And then a third. And then had to hire more staff. Everyone they knew thought they were crazy. Everyone but Andie.

She felt a sense of peace as she watched the other three talking and laughing. She'd taken the long way around, but she'd finally arrived at her destination.

Shelley Banks is a passionate writer who enjoys creating a story that will entertain readers. She is the author of three full-length novels - *One Weekend, The Diary and the Green Dress and The Long Way Around*. She is also the author of four fiction and non-fiction short reads, perfect for when you're short on time - *Short, Sweet and September, Short, Sweet and September – The Second One, Short, and Sweet and September - The Third One* and *Sweet and September - The Fourth One*.

She is also the author of September Sprouts (septembersprouts.wordpress.com), a fiction and non-fiction blog that aims to encourage people to read.

Shelley lives in Gordon Park, Queensland, Australia. You can contact Shelley via:

Facebook https://www.facebook.com/writershellb/

Instagram https://www.instagram.com/writer shellb/

www.ingramcontent.com/pod-product-compliance
Lightning Source LLC
Chambersburg PA
CBHW070532120726
47909CB00007B/2112